Will

Molly

I dedicate this book to my daughter, Hannah, who came up with the idea of mixing paranormal and thrillers. Thank you, Hannah, I'm always proud of you!!

Foreword

This is my sixth self-published book, it's not an easy option, and every day is another lesson in how difficult! I love to write, it's really that simple, and seeing my books out in the world means everything to me.

Willow Weeps came about after a suggestion from my daughter which made me wonder about combining my two loves, thrillers and horror. I hope you enjoy it, I certainly enjoyed writing it!

Are you ready? Then hold on tight, the journey is about to begin........

Chapter 1

Andrew tugged his sister's hand impatiently, and in response, Willow dragged on his arm as she stumbled, and then fell onto the floor.

Her little 5-year-old legs were unable to keep up with his lanky 10-year-old stride.

He huffed impatiently, his parents had insisted he take her with him, despite his complaints. His sister's snuffles and

hic-cupping sobs softened his irritation. Looking down at her small face and seeing the tear tracks on her grubby cheeks, he felt a wave of big brother shame.

It wasn't her fault he told himself, she just wanted to have a go on the throw-a-hoop stall and win a goldfish or a toy.

He'd had big plans when he'd seen the poster advertising the fair was in town.

It was the talk of everyone at school, but his parents had insisted on coming too, and they'd then dumped his little sister on him at the first opportunity.

Now he was having to take her along to meet his mates.

That meant no fast rides that she wasn't allowed on, and no mischief that she might inadvertently tell their parents about.

"Come on Wills, if you get a shift on, we can have a quick go at winning a goldfish."

Andrew hoped that the promise of getting her own way would make her little legs move that bit quicker.

Willow wiped her nose on her sleeve and gave a big sniff as she struggled to her feet.

"Alwight Andy, I's coming."

Digging in his pockets Andrew came across a balled-up tissue that he used to wipe her face, spitting on it first he managed to take off some of the dirt.

There wasn't much he could do about the grazes on her knees from falling over but he brushed the worst of the dirt off of her bright red shorts.

Spotting the hoopla stall he pointed it out and was rewarded by Willow's face lighting up in a wide smile.

"Come on Wills, I'll win you a goldfish."

Willow stumbled along behind him, her warm, sticky hand clutching his.

At the stall, Andrew handed over the money for two sets of hoops, one for him and one for his little sister. He lifted her up for the first go, her first two shots went wild and the third brushed one of the pegs before clattering uselessly onto the board.

Her disappointed face made him determined to live up to his role, setting her down carefully he focused on the pegs before aiming the hoop.

It landed right over it with a satisfying thud.

Taking his time to set up his throws Andrew succeeded in adding the other two hoops to the pegs. Whooping his excitement, he lifted his sister up again to see the prizes.

"Want dat one Andy."

Her little chubby finger was directed at a small, lopsided, stuffed rabbit. Its plastic eyes had been badly sewn on and were slightly skew-whiff giving it a puzzled expression. Andrew winced, it was the ugliest-looking rabbit he'd ever seen, but her heart was set on it, so he reluctantly nodded to the man behind the stall.

Willow snatched the rabbit from his hands eagerly and immediately named him "Wabbie."

Looking over at the ghost train Andrew could see that his mates were starting to gather.

"Come on Wills, my turn now."

His sister looked up at him with admiration shining in her eyes, and Andy felt 6 feet tall.

"Andy's turn now."

Willow agreed with him as they headed towards the ghost train.

Being so focused on the straggling group of his mates, Andy didn't notice Terry approaching him, until he felt a sharp shove from one side.

Losing balance, and instinctively putting out his hands to break his fall, he let go of Willow.

Andy painfully landed on his hip but managed to keep his head from hitting the ground.

He glared around to see who'd shoved him, and he immediately saw Terry looming over him.

On either side of Terry were George and Frank, or the three goons, as Andy and his mates called them.

Terry was pointing and laughing while his stupid friends joined in. Every school has a nasty bully, and Terry and his crew were it.

Tall for his age and solidly built with a squared-off face and small, cruel eyes Terry looked the part. His friends, or rather the pair of syphocants that hung around him, were the sort of kids who needed someone to follow.

George was a gangly boy whose limbs had outgrown the rest of him, and his rusty red hair was cut in an unflattering bowl shape. Frank on the other hand was a small, overweight kid, his brown hair shaved short, and his piggy eyes sunk into his doughy flesh like raisins.

Andy's friend, Derek approached, pushing his glasses up his nose in the way he always did when he was anxious.

Derek was a small, slightly built lad, his brown hair flopped over his eyes, and he impatiently brushed it back.

"You all right Andy?"

Derek reached his side and nervously shifted from foot to foot.

More of a bookish nerd than a fighter, he was clearly hoping this didn't get physical.

They were joined by the other two members of the "outsiders club."

Evan, a tall, handsome lad, with curly dark hair and sparkling blue eyes, and Steve, a fair-haired average looking boy, who came from one of the rougher estates.

Drawn together by their joint exclusion from the other kids at school they'd been friends as far back as Andy could remember.

His friends circled next to him, Steve already had his fists clenched, the scrapper of the group he was always looking for a fight.

Terry narrowed his eyes, reluctant to back down in front of his mates, but not wanting to go toe to toe with Steve in a fight he knew he'd probably lose.

"Let's leave this bunch of girls to go and play on the ghost train."

Terry's tone was derisive, but everyone knew it was more about giving himself an out and saving face.

The outsiders watched silently as the three boys turned and walked away, Steve still looking prepared to have a fight if it was needed.

Looking around, and feeling the sharp sting of panic, Andy realised his little sister wasn't where he'd thought she was.

"Wills?"

Andy could hear the anxiety in his voice when she didn't answer or come running over.

Looking around the crowds of people for her distinctive red shorts, he called out a few more times.

Picking up on his panic his friends joined in, shouting out her name and running around the area looking for her.

Heart pounding, his mouth dry, Andy started approaching people giving her description and asking if they'd seen her. One by one they shook their heads until finally, a woman pointed in the direction of the portaloos.

"I saw a small, blonde girl in red shorts and a rainbow T-shirt heading that way."

Andy felt a flood of relief, she must've needed a wee, he thought, wait until I get hold of her, wandering off like that.

The group ran over to the row of toilets, three were in use and Andy was just wondering how to find out which one contained his little sister when Evan called out to him.

Looking around he could see his friend was holding something out, and as he got closer, he could see it was a pair of small, red shorts.

Torn along the seam, and even dirtier than Andy remembered they looked as though someone had torn them off of her.

Worse than that, a dark stain spread across the hem on one side, a stain that looked suspiciously like blood.

His heart dropped like a stone into his stomach as he stared at the shorts, the whole world seemed to slow down until all he could see were those shorts.

Andy sat on the bench, hunched over by misery and shame, his head down and his chin tucked into his chest.

His parents stood together, faces twisted in worry, and he could hear his mum's muffled sobs. Andy had never felt as bad as he did right now, Willow had been in his care, and he'd failed her.

He thought about her tiny, heart-shaped face looking up at him, full of admiration for the big brother she adored.

A fat tear rolled down his cheek and dripped onto his scuffed trainers.

Feeling a weight next to him, he looked over and saw the large, plain-clothed officer had sat down. He caught a whiff of stale cigarette smoke overlaid with woody aftershave, the man's face was reassuringly calm, and his eyes were kind.

"It's not your fault son."

Andy sniffed, unconvinced and still feeling guilty, but less anxious now an adult was with him.

"I'm DCI Phelps, but call me Win. I know this is really hard on you, but I do need you to tell me again what happened."

Win handed the young boy his hanky and turned away while he wiped his eyes and blew his nose on it, shaking his head when Andy offered to return it.

"That's all right son, just keep hold of it."

"I was holding her hand, we'd just won a toy on the hoopla stall, and she was holding her stuffed rabbit in her other hand. That's when I....... sort of .....fell over."

Andy's voice trailed off at the end, and Win picked up on the first untruth the boy had told him.

Seeing the blush stain his pale cheeks Win put himself in the shoes of the ten-year-old boy he'd once been himself.

"Anything you tell me stays between us unless it's useful for finding your sister."

Andy glanced at him anxiously.

"I was pushed over, by one of the kids from school. That's when I let go of her hand, then when I looked for her afterwards, she was gone. We looked everywhere and some woman said she'd seen her going towards the toilets."

The kid fell silent as he remembered the torn, blood-stained shorts his friend had found.

"Something bad has happened to her, hasn't it?" Andy asked in a small voice.

Win patted him on the shoulder and spoke to him in a reassuring tone he didn't feel.

"We don't know that Andy, maybe she wandered off. All my officers are looking for her, and we've stopped anyone coming into or leaving the area."

DCI Phelps thought about the scene they'd found in one of the portaloos, a pile of blonde curls in the sink, and most disturbing, smears of blood on the basin. In reality, it didn't look good, and his officers had found no other trace of her despite searching every nook and cranny.

They'd just started to check all the caravans, and the fairground folk, usually unhelpful, and mistrustful of the police, had gladly thrown open their doors in a bid to find the little girl.

"Do they hate me?"

The little boy's chest hitched, and a new tear rolled down his cheek as he looked at his parents.

Win put a comforting arm around Andy.

"Of course not, they're just worried about your sister."

Andy turned his face into the policeman's broad, safe chest as more sobs racked his little shoulders.

Win's eyes fell on his mum and dad just as Andy's mum threw them a look of despair that cut his heart in two.

At only 32 he was young to make DCI, but he'd been fast-tracked, which wasn't something that made him popular with his colleagues.

He had a solve rate that had pushed him up the ladder this fast, but he had a sinking feeling this time he was out of his depth.

It felt like a house in mourning.

The curtains were drawn even though it was nearly midday casting a gloom across the room that echoed the atmosphere.

Mr & Mrs Gardner sat on the three-seater sofa, one at each end, the space between them filled with their small, downcast son.

Andy's gaze was fixed on his trainers, but his parents were looking at Win.

Their eyes were less and less hopeful each time he visited, unsurprising, he thought, as his updates were full of filler and not much in the way of new leads.

Reading his lack of progress in his face Mrs Gardner looked away, but not before he caught her scornful expression.

Since no one had invited him to sit, Win stood awkwardly in front of them like a headmaster addressing a group of wayward students outside his office.

"I'm guessing you have nothing new to add."

Jilly Gardner's voice was so heavy with bitterness and scorn that it made Win want to cringe away from her.

"I'm sorry Mrs Gardner, we've had some calls to the incident line, but nothing that's panned out."

Win thought about the sort of calls they'd had so far.

The callers ranged from people who genuinely thought they'd seen the kid to false confessions, those who made spiteful accusations against the family, and so-called psychics who claimed to have spoken to her.

The last confirmed sighting of Willow was the blonde woman at the fairground who'd seen her heading to the toilet block. Margo Granger had accurately described the girl, right down to the tatty rabbit she'd been clutching and those bright red shorts.

The only other potential lead had come from one of the fair folk, a bulky, young lad who'd been collecting tickets at the gate. He was asked if he'd seen any children leave in the timeframe between Willow being noticed missing and the police shutting down the fair.

After some thought, he'd recalled seeing a child around the same age and build, but he was adamant it couldn't have been Willow.

"It was a boy you see officer. A small boy in blue trousers and a yellow T-shirt with a smiley face on it. He had really short hair, cropped right back and a bit ragged, I remember thinking poor kid, looks as though his mum tried to do a home cut."

Win's interest rose, considering that no one knew about the hair they'd found this could easily be Willow but with her hair hacked off and in a change of clothes.

"Do you remember anything else about him? Like who he was with?"

The young man, he'd said his name was Jay, frowned with the effort of accessing the memory.

"He was really unhappy, and I mean having a full-on tantrum. Screaming and trying to pull his hand away, his mum got really angry and slapped him in the face. I was a bit taken aback. She hit him so hard I could hear it."

Win shuddered, if that was Willow then she'd almost certainly been kidnapped and assaulted, he thought back to the blood smeared on the sink.

They'd even spoken to the three lads who'd tried to pick a fight with Andy and his friends, Win had been hopeful that they'd seen something as they'd been in the area at the time. Maybe one of them had seen Willow wander off?

George, a beanpole of a boy, had stuttered and mumbled through the whole interview, his father glaring at him in ill-concealed rage that had finally spilled over when George started to cry.

"Stop that fucking baby noise boy. I told you to stop hanging around with those little shits, if you had anything to do with that kid going missing, I'll swing for yer."

George's frightened sobs had pitched to an even higher

crescendo at that point, and for the third time, Win had tried to get the man to stop scaring his son so he could get a statement out of him.

"We don't believe George had anything to do with Willow's

disappearance sir, we were simply hoping that he may have seen something that could help us."

Mr. Bellows, appropriately named, thought Win wryly, sat back in his seat and folded his arms across his chest.

He stopped having a go at George but continued to glare at him, and the kid barely managed to answer any questions after that.

Frank was a different kettle of fish.

Accompanied by his doting mother the thick-set boy had sulky muttered answers at him in a tone that Win's mother would have called "sullen."

"Dunno."

Frank shrugged dismissively at the officer and gave a deep, discontented sigh as though annoyed at the waste of his time.

Win found it difficult to hold his tongue and eventually decided some sharp words were in order.

"Don't shrug at me lad. Sit up straight and answer the questions. A small girl is missing and I'm asking you if you saw anything, less of the attitude."

Frank hadn't liked being told off, his face took on a sulky expression, but he did at least sit up a bit straighter and answer properly.

"I didn't see her; we were all looking at the losers."

When Win had glared at Frank his mother had shrugged helplessly.

"My Frankie's more of a follower officer. He's always found it hard to make friends."

Phelps wasn't surprised, he did have a small amount of sympathy for the lad, he was overweight and not terribly bright, but he was still a bully by all accounts.

It had taken a bit of time, but the boy had insisted he hadn't seen Willow after the fight with Andy and his friends. Win crossed another name off the list that seemed to get shorter and shorter by the hour.

Moving on to Terry hadn't helped matters, that one, he decided, was a budding psychopath, and probably someone he'd see a lot of in the years to come.

When he'd invited him to the station for an interview, he'd noted that the boy's father wasn't at all surprised.

He'd immediately glared at the boy and demanded to know what he'd done now, while Terry's mum had jumped to her son's defense.

Win took note of the smug look he threw at his father when he thought no one was watching.

Now he had the boy and his mother sat in front of him and Terry couldn't conceal his glee at sharing his "insights" into the case.

"I expect she was taken by some pervert. You see it all the time."

Win was shocked to see a glow of excitement on Terry's face, he was practically bouncing on his chair.

"By now he'll probably have chopped her up. Maybe he took her head off?"

Win was feeling slightly sick at the image that conjured up, what sort of kid came up with shit like that, he thought.

"Did you see her wander off Terry?"

The boy shook his head, he almost looked sorry he hadn't seen her, most likely because he was enjoying his minor role and wanted a bigger part.

"I was too busy trying to avoid getting hit by that horrible kid off the estate. Are you going to arrest him, officer? He threatened me."

Win swept over that question without responding, he'd already had chapter and verse of what had happened that night; and if anyone got nicked, it would be Terry and his mates.

Terry's mum, Mrs Elizabeth Peck, hadn't been so quick to let it go though.

"My Terry's right officer, what are you doing about those boys? Always picking on my Terry and his friends they are, horrible little deviants. They probably killed her themselves and now they're trying to blame my boy."

"I don't think now's a good time for the police to be getting involved in a playground scrap Mrs Peck. We have a missing child to find and believe me, we'll be questioning everyone and turning over every stone to find out what happened to her."

Slightly mollified by his response she turned her adoring gaze on Terry, he in turn played up to her.

He rested his head on her shoulder, but while all of her attention was on her son, his was on Win.

The cold smile that crept across his face gave him the willies, and he just knew the kid was still thinking up gory scenarios.

Andy's friends had been as helpful as they could.

Nice kids who clearly cared about Andy a great deal, they'd been out every night, walking around the area looking for Willow.

One of his officers had come across them, the small one with the glasses being given a leg up to poke through a large bin.

Their desperation to find her was written all over their faces, and the disappointment was tangible as one by one they had to admit they hadn't seen her again after the fight.

Evan was the most distressed of the bunch and Win felt his heart go out to him.

He'd found the shorts and apparently, he was waking up every night with nightmares about it.

Back in the present Win shifted uncomfortably from foot to foot and hoped no one would notice.

His feet were killing him, he'd barely been home in the last two months, chasing every lead, and pouring over the case notes for anything that had been missed.

Mr. Gardner waved at the spare armchair.

"Sit down officer, you look exhausted."

Win reluctantly refused the offer, if he sat down, he'd struggle to get back up, plus he'd be here longer than he needed to be, and he was desperate to get back to the station.

This wasn't his only case anymore.

Since the trail had gone cold his desk had started to pile up with new cases, murders, attempted murders, sexual assaults, the whole gambit of evil.

It was only his own insistence that he keep on this that had persuaded his bosses to let him keep chasing it, but he knew it wouldn't be much longer until they started pulling him off altogether.

A moment of uncomfortable silence fell, heavy and oppressive, but Win had no more for them.

The last he saw as he left their house, was the three of them, sitting in a row on that sofa, still as statues in the gloomy room.

Chapter 2

Andy's daughter was five, and her birthday had been a bittersweet moment.

Lissie was the mirror image of her aunt at the same age, and it made his heart ache to look at her sometimes. His mum didn't even try, she was distant and cold and refused to see her granddaughter.

Sometimes, he thought he saw a desperate longing in his mother's eyes, that was until the shutters came down again. It still hurt, no matter how great his life was now the lack of a relationship with his mum left a hole that no one could fill.

His parents had divorced two years after Willow's disappearance, and his dad was remarried, but his mum had stayed alone, bitter, and angry at the world.

Despite her denials, Andy knew she blamed him for Willow being taken.

Of course, no one knew for sure what had happened to her, but that seemed to be the direction all the evidence pointed in. A person or persons unknown had taken her as she walked to the toilet block at the fair.

They'd either cut off her beautiful golden curls, put her in boy's clothes, and then walked her out, right under everyone's noses, or something worse had happened to her.

Andy was never sure what scenario was for the best, the one where she'd been killed or the one where someone else had taken her.

There hadn't been a sign of her in thirty years.

Her body hadn't shown up, no clues, no sightings, nothing, every lead had led nowhere and eventually all the interest had dried up.

Every once in a while, a newspaper ran a cold case story, but it was just a rehash of the original case with nothing new to add. The woman who'd seen her heading to the toilets had given an interview each time they ran the story, enjoying her moment of glory over and over again.

He'd stopped reading them a few years ago, anger burning him at the thought of this woman who'd barely touched the case seeking the limelight and lunching out on being one of the last people to see his sister alive.

Andy had moved away from his hometown as soon as he could but leaving the memories behind hadn't been as easy.

People still recognised his last name when he was introduced, there'd be a moment of unease as they struggled with the choice of pretending they didn't know and the temptation of finding out the ghoulish details.

He'd become adroit at brushing over it and noting to himself that they were someone to avoid in future.

The only person in his new life that he'd discussed it with fully was his wife.

She'd sensitively avoided the subject the whole time they were dating, until one day, knowing they were getting serious, he'd sat her down and bought it up himself.

It hadn't been as hard as he'd thought it would be, Olive had listened without interruption and when he'd felt the tears stinging his eyes had felt her loving arms around him.

Only she knew what it did to him every day, how he lived with the guilt, the shame, of being the big brother that let his little sister down in the worst way possible.

He was pulled out of his unpleasant trip down memory lane by a pair of skinny little arms wrapping around his legs, looking down he could see the heart-shaped face of his daughter grinning up at him.

Swinging her up in his arms he whirled her around in a circle until she squealed.

"You'll make her sick," his wife, Olive, observed drily from the doorway.

Andy chuckled and lowered Lissie to the ground, where she stumbled slightly, dizzy from spinning.

"Disaster averted," he announced, as his wife shook her head in mock exasperation.

"Come on little one, time for school."

Lissie groaned theatrically and crumpled herself to the floor where she lay as still as a statue.

Olive hid a grin behind her hand.

"That's enough of that, little Miss, get yourself up or we'll be late."

After grabbing up Lissie's rucksack and lunchbox, Olive grazed a kiss across his cheek before dashing out of the door.

Andy poured himself a second coffee, he worked from home, which meant no morning commute, no rush to get ready, and best of all, hanging out in his pyjamas until lunchtime.

As a freelancer, he wrote articles on anything from politics to cooking, and everything in between.

After completing the work that had a deadline and sending it to the editors, Andy realised he only had half an hour to get himself dressed and to the café to meet his dad for lunch.

Mark Gardner was already there when he arrived, and Andy slipped into the seat opposite.

His dad's face, often serious and grim in repose, lit up when he saw his son.

Despite re-marrying five years after Willow's disappearance his dad hadn't had any more children.

His new wife had a son from a previous relationship and that was enough for his dad who doted on the lad.

Andy had never felt a moment's jealousy though, his dad had more than enough love for them both and it was heart-warming to hear him call Mark, dad.

"How are my girls?"

The pride shone from his dad's face, he loved Olive and worshipped Lissie.

Andy had seen the tears shine in his dad's eyes as he looked at his granddaughter, but he didn't let it get in the way of having a relationship with her.

Unlike his mum, he thought sadly.

"Both good, dad, Lissie wants to know if you can make it to her school for show and tell. Apparently, she's decided that showing everyone her grandad is better than anything else she can take in!"

Mark laughed, "If she insists, although god knows what I'm going to say to a bunch of expectant 5-year-olds."

They continued their catch-up as they waited for their order, Andy plumping for a chicken sandwich and his dad sticking to his usual beans on toast.

"How's Calvin?"

Andy's stepbrother had been struggling lately, he'd broken up with his girlfriend and had to move back home. At 35, he wasn't taking to it too well, and Mark had found his relationship with Cal more strained than usual.

"He's getting there. We had a heart-to-heart, and I think we cleared the air. It's definitely been less fraught since anyway."

The waitress returned, putting the plates in front of them she checked they didn't want anything else before heading to the next table.

Both men focused on their food, so comfortable with each other that they didn't feel the need to fill every gap in the conversation.

Andy had just finished his sandwich, and his dad was wiping up the last of the bean juice with some toast when someone cleared their throat behind him.

Turning around he saw a short, slim woman waiting behind him with a nervous expression.

"Andy Gardner, I need to speak to you urgently."

Andy frowned, he was sure he didn't recognise her, but she seemed to know his name.

"How can I help? Have we met? I'm sorry I don't remember you."

The woman pulled a face and sighed.

"This is where things go wrong. My name is Cleo Hart, you haven't met me before, but I have an important message for you."

This was starting to feel like a cold sell, Andy thought, either that, or there was something wrong with her.

"What message is that Mrs. Hart?"

"It's Miss, but please call me Cleo."

Andy nodded and waited for her to answer his question.

"Would you mind if I sat down? It'll be easier if I can speak to you properly and I'm drawing too much attention standing here."

His dad waved at the spare seat.

"Be our guest Cleo. Can I get you something? A coffee maybe?"

Andy shot his dad a look of exasperation, he'd rather not get her comfortable until he knew what was going on.

Cleo plonked herself in the spare chair and asked the waitress for a white coffee.

"I might need that to go" she muttered.

Both men waited in silence and eventually, Cleo let out a deep sigh.

"Right, I'll just get this over with. Do you know anyone called Willow? She's telling me you're her brother, and you're her dad."

Cleo had pointed at them one at a time, and Andy narrowed his eyes, this hadn't happened for a while, but at one point they were constantly being pestered by so-called psychics.

He dug deep, and finally found what he hoped was a patient, polite, but uninterested, tone.

"I think you know exactly who we are Cleo."

The woman winced, maybe his tone hadn't been as neutral as he'd hoped, but then he wasn't too bothered by upsetting her.

"I appreciate this might be a lot to take in, and I'm sure you had quite a few charlatans contact you over the years, which always makes it harder for those of us who are genuine."

Andy put his hand over his father's, he could feel it tremble under his touch and he felt a wave of anger at this woman who was causing him so much distress.

"You're upsetting my dad. Please leave."

Just then the waitress appeared, and apparently having heard Cleo's muttered remark earlier, had put her coffee in a cardboard carry-out cup.

Despite this, Cleo didn't move, if anything she seemed to plant herself more firmly in the seat, before removing the lid and adding condiments to her hot drink.

Stirring the contents slowly she took a moment before speaking.

"You called her "Wills" and you won her a stuffed rabbit at the fair that night. She called it "Wabbie" because she couldn't say her Rs"

Andy felt tears sting behind his eyes, and the lump in his throat choked him.

He could see Willow's face as he handed that ugly rabbit to her, the admiration that shone from her eyes. Admiration he didn't deserve, he thought bitterly, some big brother I was.

Even worse than his own emotional rollercoaster, was the growing glow of hope in his dad's eyes.

Desperate for something, anything, that told him where his daughter was, Mark had never given up hoping she was alive, and that one day she would be returned to them.

Compassion filled Cleo's eyes as she continued.

"Your friend found her shorts, but the rabbit was never found, the police found her hair in the sink in the bathroom."

"You could've got most of that from newspaper reports, the police released the information about her hair."

"But they held back the rabbit, didn't they?"

Cleo counted him easily and Andy took a shuddering breath.

She gave them both a long, sad, look.

"You need time to take it in, I'll leave you my contact details and give you space to talk. When you're ready, call me. I have a message for you, Andy, she's desperate for me to pass it on."

Laying a business card on the table, Cleo picked up her coffee and walked out of the café.

Andy looked at his dad, he'd picked up the card and was turning it around between his fingers, the hope and expectation on his face were more than Andy could bear.

"It wouldn't hurt to contact her. Just hear what she has to say, you've got to admit she knew things that no one else outside of the family knows."

Andy sighed, he knew how stubborn his dad could be, and he wasn't likely to let this drop until Andy had agreed.

Taking the card from his dad and placing it in his own wallet he nodded.

"I'll call her, but you don't need to be there. I'll let you know if she's genuine or has anything relevant to say."

His dad squeezed his son's fingers.

"You're a good boy Andy, I'm lucky to have you."

Feeling choked again Andy brushed an affectionate kiss on his dad's bristly cheek.

"I love you, dad."

The two men sat in silence while they waited for the bill, both two full of the past to speak.

Chapter 3

Andy waited impatiently for Cleo to show up.

She hadn't seemed surprised at his call, if anything she seemed to be expecting it.

The busy wine bar was near the railway station and was full of commuters having a couple of after-work drinks before going home. There was a low hum of conversation around him, and he'd found himself a table at the back of the bar where they'd have some privacy.

Cleo arrived dead on time and made a beeline for him, after ordering herself a large glass of wine.

"I'm only here because I promised my dad I'd speak to you, but you need to be aware that I am not as easily taken in."

Andy's words and tone were harsh, and Cleo's eyes widened at his bluntness before holding her hands up in front of her as though warding off an attack.

"I come in peace" she joked, but her smile fell flat as she saw his face harden.

"Probably not the best time to be making light of the situation, I tend to let my mouth run away when I'm nervous."

Taking a long gulp of her wine she crossed her legs.

"I've been able to hear these messages for as long as I can remember. As a kid, I didn't see anything wrong with it, but obviously, it's not usual and my mum made sure I knew to keep it to myself before I started school."

Cleo's face clouded over for a moment.

"I soon learned why I had to keep it to myself, I made the mistake of telling one of my teachers I had a message from her mum who'd died a few months before. She went hysterical and the school made my mum come and collect me."

"So, is everyone you hear from dead?"

Cleo could hear the pain, but also the hope, in his voice as he asked.

"Not always. I get messages from those who are distressed and in need of help, mostly they have passed on, but not always."

Andy waited, he wasn't sure what to say, she seemed very certain of herself and her "gift," but he wasn't convinced.

"Okay, so here I go. It's a name. George Bellows, Bellows like the things you blow a fire with. Does that mean anything to you? She's very angry and didn't explain."

Andy blanched.

"How do you know that name?"

Cleo brushed her long curly hair back behind her shoulders

"I told you, Willow told me, or at least that's the name she gave for herself."

Andy downed his drink and got up for another, he returned from the bar with a double shot of something dark and another pint of lager.

"George Bellows was a nasty little bully who hung around with another pair of the same ilk back when I was a kid."

Cleo nodded, as though agreeing with him, she swirled her wine around the glass as though listening to something only she could hear.

"She's letting me know that's the person she's talking about."

Andy felt intrigued despite himself.

"You're talking to her now?"

Cleo shrugged, "Not exactly talking, that would suggest we have a conversation. They tend to just give me messages with little interest in getting any response from me."

"The police spoke to him at the time and said he had nothing to do with Willow going missing."

"I don't know Andy; she hasn't given me any details just a name."

Andy frowned into his pint as though the amber liquid held all the answers.

"What do I do with it though? The police will just laugh me out of the station if I go to them with this."

He rubbed his hand across his face, his expression wary.

"I haven't been back since the day I finally left. Too many memories and none of them good."

Downing his drinks Andy straightened in his chair and rolled his shoulders.

"Maybe it's time. Time to go back and get some closure."

Getting his jacket off of the back of the chair, he gave Cleo a long, thoughtful look.

"Would you come with me? If Willow really is telling you stuff, then I'm guessing having you along will be helpful."

Swallowing down her own remaining wine she nodded reluctantly.

When he'd gone, she got herself another drink, standing at the bar while she drank, she thought about what she'd just agreed to.

A trip to a town she didn't know with a stranger who probably didn't like her too much, and no guarantee that it would lead anywhere.

She was painfully aware that if Andy didn't get results, he'd resent her for it.

She'd opened up old wounds and given him hope, she could only hope it wasn't for nothing.

Cleo stepped out of the shower, she hadn't heard a peep out of Willow since she'd met up with Andy the night before.

Maybe with George's name passed on and Andy planning to return to town, she'd got what she needed.

Wrapping a towel around herself she glanced at the steamed-up mirror over the sink.

George Bellows

His name was written in steam, but just in case she hadn't got the message it also reverberated through her head like an earworm song.

"Alright, alright. I told him, what more do you want?"

George Bellows

Cleo winced, the voice was sharp and high, like claws scratching on a blackboard. Rubbing the mirror clean with the palm of her hand Cleo turned to walk away until she heard the squeak of a finger on the mirror.

Find him

The high-pitched voice bounced the two words around her brain, over and over, Cleo held her hands over her ears, but of course, it made no difference.

Picking up the phone she dialed the number for Andy, until she passed it on she knew she'd get no peace tonight.

When Andy hung up on Cleo he made another call, one that he hadn't made for a long time, but it was still a number he knew by heart.

"Derek, hi it's Andy."

The explanations hadn't been easy, but to his credit, Derek didn't mock him once.

"If you think it's worth a look then I'm with you mate. Outsiders to the end."

Derek had insisted that Andy stay with him while he was in town, and Andy was grateful, if he was going back, then he was going to need all his friends around him.

Telling Olive had felt more difficult.

They hadn't lied to each other once in all the years they'd been married, and Andy didn't intend to start now.

They sat on the bed, in the room where they'd shared every piece of news, good and bad, over the years. The familiar wallpaper, dotted with little flowers, the clunky old wardrobe that Olive loved too much to replace, and the dresser where she did her make-up before they went out.

It was comfortable and reassuring, and for a moment he almost backed out, desperately just wanting to stay here, safe and warm with his wife.

He told her the whole, unbelievable, crazy tale from start to finish, and when he was done, she got up and threw her arms around him.

"You've got to go, what choice do you have? If there's any chance, even the smallest one that you can find out what happened to Willow, you have to take it."

That was Olive all over, he thought, always putting him first, and always cheering him on.

"I'll get off first thing in the morning, I've written Derek's number on the pad by the phone."

Olive nodded before getting up, she started to pull down the large suitcase from on top of the wardrobe, frowning as she realised it was coated in a film of dust.

"I'm a shitty housewife."

Andy managed a chuckle, "I didn't marry you for your housekeeping skills"

Olive turned in his arms, so she was facing him.

"And what did you marry me for?"

Her tone was light and teasing, Andy ran his hand down the small of her back and pulled her close.

"Oh, I don't know, this and that I guess."

Olive playfully slapped his arm, "Teach me to dig for compliments."

Ducking out from under his arms she began opening drawers and fetching out various clothes and folding them into his case.

"I want to say hurry home, but I also want you to take your time, get this sorted once and for all, and come back when you're sure you've done everything you can."

Andy ducked his head and pretended to be checking his toiletries bag to hide the tears that had welled up and were threatening to spill down his cheeks.

His heart felt as though it would burst with the love he felt from his wife.

Just before he zipped up his bag, he added two last items from the bedside cabinet.

A large, framed photo of Willow and him, and a snapshot of him with Derek, Evan, and Steve.

He didn't know why, but it suddenly felt important to take it.

Andy looked at it before zipping up his case, the four of them had their arms around each other, Steve's face was turned to Evan, Derek's finger was on the front of his glasses as though he'd just pushed them up, and he was facing the camera with a wide smile across his face.

He remembered that day as if it was yesterday, the boys had been to his house for a BBQ, and his dad had lined them up in front of the house for a photo.

It was one of the last good days, three short weeks before Willow was taken, and their lives had changed forever.

No more BBQs, no more friends over for visits, the house was too quiet and too dark.

His mum moved through the rooms like a shadow of herself, never settling in one place for long, she walked slowly, but purposefully.

Occasionally she'd stop at a photo of Willow, and she'd run her finger across the glass as though by doing so she could touch the child she'd lost.

Her face became drawn, a pale version of who she once was, her eyes sunken and ringed by dark smudges.

Jilly rarely slept more than an hour or two at a time, she was waiting, always waiting, waiting for her child to come home to her.

His dad had tried his best, he'd try to hold her, to offer comfort, but she'd push him away.

Andy saw the sting of rejection in his father's eyes every day.

As for him, she did the basics.

He was fed, clothed, and helped with his homework; she'd feigned interest in his day but wouldn't listen when he answered her.

Sometimes he was sure he could feel resentment in her stare, an aura that she felt she'd lost the wrong child, or that she blamed him for losing Willow.

He tried to stay in touch with her, but every conversation was painful and awkwardly polite.

Being in town, he'd have no choice but to visit her, she'd soon find out he was there, and he dreaded it.

Jilly still lived in the family home, she refused to leave, clinging to the hope that one day her daughter would come back, and she'd need to know where to find her.

Sighing, he closed the case and pulled it off the bed before wheeling it into the corner of the room.

The past he'd run from was racing towards him like a derailed train and he couldn't shake the feeling that he was making the wrong choice by going back.

Chapter 4

The town hadn't changed much in the decades since he'd left.

A few new shops, chain pubs and cafes, and more housing, but it was still similar enough to evoke memories.

The corner where the Outsiders used to meet up, the park where they hung out, and the large council-owned field where the fair had set up that fateful day.

Andy screeched to a halt.

Cleo, who'd traveled down with him, jerked against her seatbelt but bit back the rebuke she'd been about to deliver when she saw what he was looking at.

On the telegraph pole outside the field was a giant poster with a manically smiling clown pasted across the center.

The Fairground is in town!

His eyes were fixed on the poster, was it a coincidence?

It would be exactly 30 years later when it opened.

Thirty years since Andy had been a ten-year-old boy, excited to be meeting up with his mates and looking forward to trying out the rides.

Thirty years since he'd let his sister's hand slip out of his, and she'd been lost forever.

Seeing the compassion burning in Cleo's eyes, Andy managed a watery smile in her direction.

"Sorry, I didn't mean to almost decapitate you with the seatbelt! I'm okay, it was just a bit of a shock that's all."

Cleo turned to face him.

"I can't help but feel there's a reason we've been led back here, are you really up to this?"

Andy nodded, he met her eye, and even though he could feel his heart pounding with fear he swallowed it down.

"I can do this Cleo."

He glanced one last time at the poster, to him the clown seemed more menacing than amusing, but maybe that was just because of the history.

"There's someone I want to speak to before we go to Derek's, a woman named Margot Granger. She saw Willow headed to the toilets that night, maybe there was something else that she didn't think was important at the time?"

Putting the car back into gear he pulled away, he'd looked up Mrs. Granger before leaving and knew exactly how to get to her house.

Mrs. Margot Granger's hair was still blonde, thanks to a bottle rather than nature, thought Cleo.

She was plump and squashed into a too-small dress that ended at her knees, makeup settled in the sags and wrinkles of a face aged by 30 years but pretending not to be.

The woman had greeted the pair enthusiastically, assuming initially they were journalists.

Preening on the doorstep she'd quoted her fee in a way that suggested this was a tried and practiced routine for her.

"It's £250 for a quote, another £100 on top if you need me to go over the original events and it'll be a total of £700 if you'd like a new photo to go with the article. I've noticed the fairs in town so maybe we can do one under the sign? That should prompt some renewed interest."

Andy swallowed his disgust; Willow had just become a cash cow for this woman.

He noticed the way her face dropped when he announced who he was, he introduced Cleo as a friend rather than going into details about her real involvement.

Margot reluctantly waved them in, her house was neat as a pin and the walls were decorated by framed newspaper articles of all the stories, she'd taken part in.

She had the decency to blush when she saw Andy looking at them.

Seeing his sister's smiling face staring down from the walls was disconcerting, every article featured the same photo, the one that his parents had shared with the world when they still thought they had a chance to find her. It was her first school picture, and to Andy looked unnatural and posed.

"How can I help you, Andy?"

The woman's familiarity irritated him, in fact, everything about her did.

"I need to hear exactly what you saw the night Willow went missing, just in case anything comes to you that didn't seem important at the time."

What had sounded logical in the car earlier suddenly sounded hollow to his own ears and from the expression on Margot's face, she was thinking much the same.

"OOOO is there a breakthrough in the case? Something new?"

Her excitement made him feel queasy, he could see the eagerness lighting up her eyes at the thought of having something new to share, and then the disappointment when he shook his head.

"Nothing new Mrs. Granger. It's thirty years since my sister went missing and I'd just like to get everything clear in my own head."

Margot shrugged before moving into what sounded like a well-practiced spiel.

"I'd just got myself a drink and was looking for my friend when I noticed the little girl, what stood out was that she seemed to be too small to be on her own. She had curly blonde hair, was wearing red shorts, and a rainbow T-shirt, and holding a really strange-looking stuffed rabbit. I was going to approach her and find out if she was lost, but she looked happy enough, swinging her toy as she skipped along in the direction of the toilets."

Cleo could see the clouds of anger across Andy's face and took over the questioning.

"And you definitely didn't see anyone else approach her at all?"

Margot shook her head, the disappointment at not having more to tell etched across her face.

"No one, but then I didn't look at her for long, once I was sure she looked okay I carried on looking for my friend until Andy and his friends approached me looking for her. Believe me, I've racked my brain for anything else I can add but there was nothing."

I bet you have, thought Cleo, I bet you've wished and wished there was a way you could play an even bigger role than you already do.

Andy was drumming his fingers on his leg as he eyed Margot with irritation.

"It didn't occur to you that a five-year-old shouldn't be wandering around a fairground on her own?"

Margot flushed, the heat from her face melting the thick layer of foundation causing beige sweat to trickle down her chin and streak her mottled neck.

"Hindsight's a great afterthought young man. How was I supposed to know at the time?"

Her voice was sharp with annoyance, this was a woman who didn't feel she deserved to be questioned.

Her entitled attitude pushed Andy's annoyance up a peg.

"You've certainly made good out of my sister over the years Mrs. Granger, how do you think her family feels every time you parade your small, insignificant role all over the press?"

Margot narrowed her piggy eyes, Andy's words causing annoyance, not guilt.

"I think you two should leave now."

Andy nodded in agreement

"Absolutely Mrs Granger, being here with you makes me sick to my stomach so I'll be pleased to get away. Just note, that I don't expect the papers to be printing up a story on my visit today."

From the sudden blotching of colour on her cheeks, it was clear that was exactly what Mrs. Granger had intended to do.

Hoping that what he'd said would be enough to discourage her Andy and Cleo eagerly took their leave.

Derek was now a well-paid, successful, and wealthy, game designer.

He stood out on his front porch watching for them, his round face lit up with anticipation and it wasn't until he saw his old friend that Andy realised how much he'd missed him.

The two men fell into each other arms without any hesitation, or discomfort, their old relationship still felt as strong as it had over thirty years ago when they first met.

Derek stepped back; his smile spread from one cheek to the other.

"What do you think of the new look? Contacts instead of those god-awful glasses."

Andy drank in the sight of the best friend he'd ever had.

"You look great."

At that, his voice cracked, and he ducked his head to hide the tears he felt stinging the back of his eyes.

He'd known it would be emotional, but he hadn't prepared himself for just how much it would affect him seeing his friend after so long.

Clearly aware of his friend's discomfort, Derek waved them both into the large, imposing house behind him. It loomed behind the gravel drive that was only accessed by automatic gates and walking in Andy could see it was as huge inside as it was out.

Their footsteps echoed in the oversized hallway and Derek blushed, looking embarrassed by the ostentatious surroundings.

Andy decided a bit of good-natured teasing might put him at his ease.

"Someone did okay for themselves! I'm guessing there's plenty of room for us guests, I just hope you're not expecting us to get all fancied up for dinner."

Derek chortled and then threw his head back in a full, belly laugh.

"Stop taking the piss you."

As though to underline his wealth, and make the situation even more hilarious, a bland-faced man in his late fifties appeared.

"I'm Reynolds, I'll take your bags to your rooms."

Andy and Derek began laughing hysterically, Andy's stomach hurt, but every time he looked at his friend they were off again.

Reynolds eyed them distastefully and held out his hands for the bags, Cleo, who'd managed with a lot of effort to keep a straight face, handed her case over first.

Andy managed to push it towards Reynold's with his toe, the austere man bent over reluctantly and picked it up as though collecting dog waste off the lawn.

At his expression, Andy creased up again and Derek joined in, Reynolds, who'd clearly had enough of their silliness, turned sharply and marched off up the stairs.

Cleo shook her head.

"I dread to think what you two were like as ten-year-olds."

"We were an absolute nightmare."

Derek managed to choke this out around his laughter, finally getting hold of himself he led them into a large, tastefully decorated room.

The walls and floors were a pale cream, but the furniture and artwork added splashes of green.

"At the risk of setting off another wave of hilarity, Reynold's will fetch us all coffee when he gets down."

Andy nudged him playfully on the arm.

"Get you, a butler and a big posh house. I'm guessing you made a mint when you sold your gaming company?"

Derek nodded; he blushed bright red up the roots of his brown hair.

"Yeah, I did okay."

They all leaned gratefully back into the soft cushions of the sofas, Andy caught sight of a photo on the sideboard, it was the same one he had in his bag, all four of them in his garden together.

"What's happened to the others? I haven't heard from any of them for quite a while now."

"Evan's doing okay, he's been married and divorced more times than any man has a right to be, but he's got a good job as a journalist. Steve, now that's a sad one. He's had a few spells in prison over the years. Been out for a while now, and said he's not going back, but we'll see. With a few drinks in him, he gets into fights. I do what I can to help him out, and Evan got him a job at the paper."

Derek got up and fetched the photo over.

"You guys were all I had. You were my family."

His face clouded with memories.

1988

At five years old, Derek was small for his age.

His black-rimmed glasses were too big for his tiny face and constantly slipped down his nose.

They'd broken in the middle at some point and a well-meaning member of staff at the children's home had stuck them together with tape.

Derek was in care, he didn't remember being removed from his mum at two, and all he knew was that she couldn't look after him.

The staff were kind enough, but it wasn't like having a family of his own.

It didn't take long for word to get around the school about him.

The weather was mild for late September, and Derek was planning to sit and read his new book on the bench.

He'd not made any friends yet, but he was happy with a book and his own company.

As he made his way across the playground, he wasn't concerned with anything or anyone apart from the imaginary world of reading.

Next thing he knew, he was flying through the air, landing with a thump on the ground that winded him, and he looked up to see a large, leering face staring down at him.

"Oi care kid. You don't belong here, there should be a special place for rejects like you."

Derek felt around next to him, his glasses had come off, and everything was blurry without them.

"This what you're looking for?"

A foot prodded him in the side, and a new, mocking voice joined the other one.

Squinting, Derek could see the outline of a plump kid waving something in his hand, something that he assumed were his glasses.

He winced when he heard a sharp, snapping noise, it wasn't likely he'd get a replacement pair any time soon, and without them he was blind as a bat.

"Leave him alone."

This voice sounded a little anxious, but he heard footsteps running towards him, and then a pair of arms hefting him to his feet.

"What are you boys up to?"

The commanding voice of the headmaster cut across the playground; all seven boys immediately muttered "Nuffing sir."

Derek's sight cleared as someone placed his glasses back on his nose, they hung down on his left ear where they'd been snapped by whoever had hold of them earlier.

"I've got a bit of sticky tape in my bag; I reckon I could fix them."

A scruffy lad with a roughly shaven head and a misfitting uniform was already digging through a battered rucksack.

He looked up with a triumphant grin as he waved the small roll of tape in the air.

Handing the roll to a dark-haired lad to do the repair the scruffy one held out his hand to shake.

"I'm Steve, the one doing the fixing is Evan, and that one's Andy."

Derek shared his name, nervously pushing his freshly repaired glasses back up his too-small nose so he could see his new friends clearly.

"Who were the other ones?"

The one called Andy pulled a face, the one you make when you're made to eat your vegetables, thought Derek.

"That's Terry, George, and Frank. They like picking on people."

Evan nudged Derek's shoulder.

"Come on, let's go kick a ball about until the whistle goes."

The four boys headed off together, and for the first time, Derek felt a part of things, as though he belonged somewhere.

Back in the present Derek gently put the photo down on the coffee table between them.

"So, I think we need to get everyone over here, we were all there that night, and we should all get involved in whatever this is that's happening now."

Andy nodded, "And what about George Bellows? We should find out what happened to him as well, it's his name that keeps coming up."

Derek unfolded a laptop and pressed the pad to bring it back to life.

"I took the liberty of doing a bit of research online. It would seem that George still lives with his dad, a caretaker at the school has never been married, and has no children."

Spinning the laptop around he showed Cleo and Andy the school website where a photo of all the staff headed the home page. George was still rail-thin, his pinched face looked weaselly, and he was the only one not attempting to smile.

Andy stared at his one-time nemesis; it was hard to believe he'd ever been scared of him.

"Strange to think he works in our old school."

Derek nodded, "Almost as though he's been held back in time, isn't it? Anyway, you guys need to go unpack and freshen up. I'll call the others and get them over as soon as possible."

Andy and Cleo stood up as Reynolds walked into the room, spooky, thought Andy, almost as though he knew we needed him.

He was still eying them with an air of disapproval Andy noted.

"Follow me."

Andy had just finished putting his things away and was debating if there was time for a quick cat nap on that massive king-sized bed when he heard Cleo scream next door.

Running to her room he barely knocked before bursting in and seeing her in just a towel, fresh out of the shower, he mumbled an embarrassed apology.

Cleo was too busy staring at the mirror to care, her face was pale, and she pointed a trembling finger at the steam.

George Bellows
FIND HIM

Andy stepped back, it was one thing hearing about this stuff, but another to be witnessing it. Cleo wiped the words away with a flannel

"I thought once we got here, she'd stop."

Andy shrugged, "Maybe once we've seen him, she will."

Realising that she was wearing just a towel Cleo flushed, and Andy hastily excused himself.

Back in his room, he ran it through his head again, what did George have to do with his sister, and if it was her sending those messages, why was she so desperate for them to speak to him?

Chapter 5

Margot Granger closed down the call with a satisfied smirk.

The editor of the local paper, Neil Little, had almost bitten her hand off for the story about the missing kid's brother showing up at her house asking questions.

Margot had used a little "artistic licence" with her description of the visit and was already planning how it would sound in her head.

She needed to add tears and distress, she thought, it wouldn't work if she didn't ramp up the emotional value.

Margot rubbed her hands together in an unconscious movement that showed the glee she felt at the thought of the money she'd make from having a new story to sell.

Requests from the papers had dried up to almost nothing in the last ten years and her small circle of friends had heard the details of her role so many times since it happened, they were sick of hearing it.

She'd needed a new angle and look how one had dropped in her lap.

Catching a glance at herself in the mirror she decided to re-do her make-up, it was looking a bit smudged, she thought.

While upstairs she checked her image in the full-length mirror, hmmm, it might be an idea to refresh the outfit too, she thought.

Margot opened her wardrobe and scrutinised the contents, it was looking to be another hot day so nothing that would make her sweat too much. Her eye caught on a strappy dress;

the floaty material was flattering to her shape but would also keep her cool.

Hurriedly changing before re-doing her make-up Margot added a pair of heeled sandals to the outfit. Spinning around in front of the mirror she admired her reflection, to Margot she looked fabulous, she didn't see that the dress was too short and revealed too much of her plump white thighs.

Margot was already calculating what her new story was worth, surely, she could ask a lot more for this one, she thought eagerly. The phone ringing from downstairs made her start, it was probably Neil calling back.

Hurrying as fast as she could on the high heels she raced to the top of the stairs, but before she could take the first step, she swore she felt a cold hand on the small of her back.

A sharp shove and she lost her footing, her heel tangled in the carpet pile and the shoe was ripped off her foot as she tumbled down the staircase.

Margot reached out her hand, trying to grab the banister as she went.

At one point she almost got a hold, but the momentum of her fall meant all she succeeded in doing was snapping her fingernail on the hardwood.

What had only taken seconds in reality, felt much longer to Margot as she felt every carpet burn, and every time she smashed her head against the wall or banister.

It was almost a relief when she heard the sharp crack of her neck breaking just before she thudded to the floor in the hall.

The four of them were in a room together for the first time in nearly thirty years.

Evan was sprawled across one of the deep-cushioned armchairs and sipping from a glass half filled with a dark liquid. He'd grown into a handsome man; time had added some lines to his face and grey shot through the once-dark hair. His blue eyes still twinkled with good humour, and Andy noticed that he shot Cleo an appreciative glance or three.

Steve on the other hand looked tired, drawn, and old before his time. He was wandering around the room, lifting and then closely inspecting various ornaments, Andy noticed his arms were inked with what looked like "prison tattoos." A bottle of lager was in his hand, and he swigged from it at regular intervals.

They'd greeted each other warmly, the years falling away as they'd hugged.

Andy had then introduced them all to Cleo and given them an account of what had bought him back to the town he'd turned his back on as soon as he'd been able to.

Evan seemed to take it all at face value, but Steve had glared suspiciously at the woman sitting to one side of the group.

"What's in it for you love?"

His hard eyes hadn't wavered from her face, Andy recognised that expression, it was Steve preparing for a confrontation, and he intervened quickly.

"Cleo knows things that the police didn't release, like Willow's shorts that Evan found. I know how it sounds mate, but I have to know what happened to her."

Steve had softened, only slightly, but Andy could sense that the danger had passed.

Cleo had kept quiet through their exchange but now she spoke.

47

"We need to speak to George Bellows, I don't know any more than that, but we need to speak to him. Maybe there was something he didn't share with the police at the time?"

Evan shrugged.

"Him and that whole group of three were arseholes, but they were ten years old, if they'd seen anything surely at least one of them would've told the police."

Steve, who was still prowling around the room, snorted.

"If they'd done something wrong, why would they speak to the police? Maybe they were just worried they'd be in trouble for what they did to us, or maybe it was something worse?"

"It's all speculation at the end of the day. Until we talk to George, we won't know what it is"

While Andy was speaking, Derek had been tapping at his laptop, he looked up and cleared his throat.

"I thought while we were tripping down memory lane we may as well find the other two nasty bastards. The problem is, Frank Monroe has vanished, with no presence online at all. Terry Peck, on the other hand, he's the headmaster of our old school. I know, get that!"

Cleo frowned, pushing her hair back off her face she leaned over the laptop screen.

"So, Terry is headmaster at the school where George works as a caretaker?"

Derek nodded.

"Interesting point. It's too late to do anything tonight but we should get on it first thing tomorrow. How shall we approach George? Catch him at his house before he leaves for work?"

The others nodded their agreement, they were staying over at Derek's to make it easier to set off the next day so knowing he wasn't driving, Evan refilled his glass.

Steve helped himself to another bottle of lager, expertly popping the lid before continuing to restlessly pace the floor.

"Bloody hell Steve, can't you sit down and chill out? You're making me dizzy!"

Evan waved his hand at the empty seat next to him and Steve reluctantly sat in it but looked uncomfortable.

There was an awkward silence that Derek broke.

"Come on, let's catch up and drink my bar dry, we should be enjoying back together."

Evan lifted his glass in agreement, "To the Outsiders."

The others joined in and soon they'd started sharing news, which in Evan's case meant trying to find out more about Cleo from the lady herself.

When Evan's phone rang, he moved away from the others to take it, and after a short conversation, he came back with a grim expression.

"That was my editor, Neil, apparently, he had a call from Margot Granger earlier offering him first dibs on a story about her getting a visit from the "distraught brother of missing Willow Gardner." Ring any bells, Andy?"

Andy winced, "Me and Cleo went over there before coming here, I should've known she'd try and sell it to the papers."

Evan smiled, "It's squashed mate so don't worry. Neil tried to call her back earlier and let her know he wasn't taking her up on it but no answer."

Andy sighed with relief and thanked his mate.

"I could do without being the focus of everyone's attention right now!"

They soon got back to hitting the drinks and catching up on the intervening years and time seemed to fly by.

Finally, at just gone midnight, Andy stood up and announced he was off to bed, and the others quickly followed suit.

He lay in bed, staring at the ceiling trying to get off to sleep while listening to the muffled sounds of everyone getting ready for bed.

All he could see was his sister's face, just as it had been that night, grubby and tear stained.

"If you're out there Willow, I'll find you," he promised.

Breakfast had been a subdued affair, hastily eaten and with little in the way of conversation.

Splitting up into two cars, Derek, Steve and Evan led the way while Andy and Cleo followed on.

George's house was the middle terrace in the street, with a small, walled-off front porch and a front door that would once have been green before the paint started peeling off.

They ended up standing in a line on the narrow path with Derek at the front, allocated the one to knock and try and talk their way in.

He pressed the doorbell and waited, tapping his foot impatiently when no one came to open the door, pushing it again and following up with a sharp rat-a-tat with the door knocker. By this time Steve had shuffled out of the line and was trying to peer through the grubby, grey net curtains across the large bay window.

Bending and bobbing his head he eventually found a crack big enough to see through.

His sharp intake of breath caught the attention of the group, he stumbled backward, fell over a discarded, broken plant pot, and landed on his arse on the ground.

Derek, hemmed in by the front door, couldn't move to get to him but Evan managed to manoeuvre himself over. Steve's face was leeched of colour, and he raised a trembling finger to point at the window.

"I think you'll find he's in no state to answer the door."

After yanking Steve to his feet Evan clambered over to the window and peered through himself before urgently beckoning the others.

Andy got there first, bending almost double he peeked into what looked like the living room. It looked as though someone had turned the room over.

That, or the Bellow's family were exceptionally untidy and usually left everything scattered across the floor. George was slumped on an armchair, his long arm hanging over the side above a large pool of blood.

"Shit, shit, shit." Andy cursed out loud.

Evan had already pulled out his mobile phone and could be heard requesting an ambulance and the police. Not wanting to stay where they were, the group straggled out onto the pavement and sat in a line on the low brick wall with their backs to George's house.

"Do you think we were supposed to find him like that?"

Steve still sounded shaky, and he kept his head ducked low to hide the fear on his face.

Andy shook his head and then shrugged.

"Or this was to stop him talking to us."

Derek had hopped back off the wall and was now pacing up and down in front of them.

"What do we tell the police when they get here? We need to be singing from the same hymn sheet."

Evan nodded.

"It's not as though we can tell them a missing child spoke to mystic Meg here, they'll cart us off to the locked ward, or worse think we had something to do with it. How about just saying that we're having a reunion and wanted to catch up with George? It's not as though the police will know we hated his guts."

They all agreed, and just in time, as the wail of sirens sounded in the distance.

DCI Oliver Brooks took in the five of them with a glance and turning to the nearest uniform he instructed her to make sure they didn't go anywhere until he'd had a chance to speak to them.

The door was in such a poor level of disrepair that it only took a few hard nudges with his shoulder to put it through.

The hall was dusty and cluttered, Oliver felt his nose tickle, and try as he might, he couldn't hold back the sneeze.

The living room door was ajar, through the crack he could see a slither of the living room, papers, and possessions were scattered all over as though a petulant toddler had thrown a tantrum in there.

The body was half propped on the armchair, George Bellows had slid down the seat enough that his head was only just on the back and his legs stretched across the ground. There was a sizeable pool of blood soaking into the carpet and from the gaping wounds in George's arms. DCI Brooks didn't need a pathologist to tell him where it had come from.

Talk of the devil, thought Oliver as he heard the door open and the pathologist, Jonathan McKenzie, stride through.

"Suicide" McKenzie announced as though making a proclamation.

"That's your job to determine but if I might be so bold as to suggest that you actually examine the body first?"

McKenzie grunted, bending over the body he carefully took the victim's left arm in his gloved hand turned it over, and checked the deep wounds.

"See here? Those are hesitation cuts. This chap, or whoever cut him, wasn't too sure at first and didn't cut too deeply. Then we come to the main wound, that's deep, the blade would've cut right through the arteries, and he'd have bled out pretty quickly after that."

Oliver indicated the floor, "That look like the knife to you?"

McKenzie shrugged, "No way of telling until we do a proper comparison but I'm guessing so, he'd have dropped it about there so it would make sense."

DCI Brooks stepped back and took in the view of the whole room.

"Looks like someone turned the place over."

McKenzie took his own, cursory glance around.

"That's your job Brooks, mine is simply to give you the facts the body throws up to me. Anyway, I've got an accidental fall down the stairs waiting back at the morgue, and she'll need a PM before this chap arrives."

McKenzie sighed; he could do without a case that had too many curve balls at the moment. His wife had just left him, his dog was on its last legs, and he was only a few months off retirement.

Outside the motley crew that had called the body in were still sitting in a line on the wall, standing in front of them like a teacher lecturing his pupils he asked them to explain what they'd been doing here in the first place.

"We're having a reunion; we were mates at school and George was one of our peers. We thought we'd pop over before he started work and find out if he fancied meeting up with us later."

The speaker was a nerdy-looking bloke, Brooks noticed that he kept touching the top of his nose as though pushing up glasses even though he wasn't wearing any.

The others seemed to defer to him.

A tall, dark-haired man that Brooks thought looked familiar, Steve Birch, a man he'd arrested personally a couple of times, a woman, and another man who for some reason tweaked Brook's antenna.

Birch looked at him in mutual recognition, clearly uncomfortable about their shared history, Brooks made sure he gave him a look back that showed that he recognised him but didn't make any further comment.

"Names please."

One by one they announced their names, which reminded him why he knew the dark-haired guy. Evan Styles, the local journo, Steve Birch, the ex-offender, and Derek Lyons, a self-made gaming millionaire.

Those three were famous locally, all for different reasons, the woman he definitely didn't know, Cleo Hart, but Andy Gardner, now that was a name that was familiar for all the wrong reasons.

He was the brother of that kid that went missing at the fair thirty years ago. He'd been a wet behind-the-ears uniform back then, guarding the scene and interviewing random witnesses that weren't deemed important enough for the detectives. The senior in charge of that case had been DCI Phelps, and that had been the only case he'd retired with unclosed.

Pointing at Cleo, Brooks picked her out.

"You didn't go to school round here, what's your connection with this"

He noted that Cleo gave Andy a glance before she answered and made a mental note to himself that those two had a link of some description.

"I'm here with Andy."

He sensed she was telling him the truth, just not the whole truth, there was definitely more to it than that.

"Are we free to go, detective?"

This came from Evan, and when he nodded, they all jumped down off the wall in tandem.

Watching them walk back to their cars he frowned, he'd give a month's wages to know what they'd really been doing here this morning.

Chapter 6

It was a subdued group that got together back at Derek's place.

All eyes were on Cleo as though they believed she held the key; she shook her head at their expectant faces

"I have no idea what's going on people. My gut feeling is that we were being guided to find his body, but I haven't got a clue why."

Andy pulled Derek's laptop over the table and tapped at the keys before spinning it around for the rest of the group to see what he'd been looking up.

"DCI Phelps, retired. He's still local according to this, we're relying on our childhood memories but maybe he can help us, he spoke to everyone involved."

Derek rummaged in a drawer and pulled out a bright yellow post-it notepad where he scrawled the address for DCI Phelps before sticking it on the front of the pad he'd been making notes in.

"Any other suggestions?"

Derek looked around the room, and Steve gave Andy a long look.

"You won't like this mate, but I think you need to speak to your mum."

Andy closed his eyes for a moment, memories rushing in too fast.

He hadn't thought about his childhood after Willow for a long time, and now all the familiar feelings of guilt flooded in. Logically he knew Steve was right, but he couldn't help but feel resentful that he'd bought it up.

"I know what you're saying Steve, it's just that you guys didn't see her again afterwards, she isn't the person you all remember. I haven't seen her for a long time, we stay in touch with the odd call and message. She's bitter, dark, and angry."

Cleo's gift often gave her too much insight into people's emotions, and she could feel the waves of pain interspersed with a child's longing for his mum's approval coming off of Andy.

Steve awkwardly patted him on the shoulder, he'd never been a particularly tactile boy, but the passing years had made him even less so.

Andy pulled out his phone, glancing around the group, seeing their faces so full of sympathy for him gave him the courage to press the contact that would connect him to his mum. Getting up and walking out of earshot he listened to it ring out several times before she finally picked up.

Despite being able to see on the screen that it was her only child calling she still answered with a query in her voice, and Andy could hear the underlying spark of hope. After all of these years, she still waited for that one call that would bring her daughter home.

"Hello?"

"Hi mum, it's me. I'm in town visiting Derek and thought maybe we should get together?"

The line was silent, he knew she hadn't hung up because he could hear her breathing.

"Are you alone or is your family with you?"

The question was blunt, and his mum carefully avoided using his wife or daughter's names.

"I'm alone, Olive has work and Lissie can't take time off school. They're both fine, thanks for asking."

He heard the bitterness in his own voice, no matter how old he got her casual rejection of his family still stung.

The comment seemingly didn't penetrate, Jilly Gardner hadn't had the space for other people's emotions since she'd lost her daughter.

"When were you thinking?"

Andy didn't know why her lack of desire to see him still stung but it did.

"Today? I could drive over this afternoon."

There was silence again as though his mum was weighing up if she could get out of it, finally, he heard her sigh deeply as though put out.

"It'll have to be 2 pm, I'm hosting a meeting at four and need to set up the living room for everyone."

Andy bit his tongue; he knew exactly who she meant. He hadn't known they were still around.

The MBNF group, Missing But Not Forgotten, was a straggling group of desperate people who all had someone who had vanished and not been found. They took turns in hosting the monthly meetings, and Andy would rather not be at the house when they came.

He remembered when she'd first started it up, he'd been 12, and it was two years since his sister had gone missing.

The atmosphere at home was already thick with his mother's despair, but that was nothing compared to having nine other distressed, bitter, angry people crying in their living room. Andy would lock himself in his room, turn his music up as loud as he could get away with, and try to block out the wails of distress and the angry voices sharp with bitterness.

His father had given up by then, he'd become a quiet shadow of a man, shoulders slumped, and head bowed low. It wasn't until he'd left that some semblance of the man he'd once been had returned.

Avoiding making comments, Andy knew from past experience that to do so was pointless, he agreed to be there at 2 pm.

Awkwardly saying goodbye, he hung up, feeling guilty about his feeling of relief that the conversation was over.

DCI Unwin Phelps (retired) squinted at the jigsaw puzzle in front of him, pulling down his glasses he peered closely at the remaining pile of colourful shapes.

Someone had told him that doing puzzles kept your brain active, but he wasn't sure he had the patience for it.

The more he forced himself to spend at least an hour a day on it the bigger his urge to upend the table it sat on.

Win was sure the satisfaction of watching all those ridiculously small pieces scatter across the room would be worth the hassle of trying to pick them all up afterwards.

He glanced at the clock on the wall, another half an hour and he'd have done his "puzzle hour" and he could move on to his next "task" which was the scintillating job of putting on the laundry.

At the sound of a car, and then another, stopping outside his bungalow, he froze in place as he listened with an ex-detective's ear.

One Ford Focus, and the distinctive purr of a Jag he decided. The car doors slammed shut behind the occupants getting out, front and back doors, he noted so more than one person per car.

Always aware that his past occupation might still bring danger to his door he placed the puzzle piece back in the pile and picking up a small, hefty baton he crept over to his front door where he used the peephole to see who was approaching his home.

Four men and a woman had grouped together at the end of his path just outside his gate. He was too far away to see all of them clearly, but a couple of faces looked familiar.

Gripping his weapon tighter he wondered if that was because he'd arrested them, perhaps they were here seeking revenge. He watched as the nerdy-looking guy pushed open his gate and walked through followed by the others, they looked anxious and Win's gut instinct told him they weren't here to do him harm.

Deciding that taking control was the best option he swung the front door open before they got to it.

The nerdy one jumped back slightly before regaining his composure.

Phelps took in their faces at a glance, Steve Birch jumped out at him, he'd spent his early career nicking his dad and then the son not long before retirement.

He did a double take on the tall, fair-haired man with sad eyes.

"Andrew Gardner. What brings you to my door?"

Andy held out his hand to shake, he had to lean around Derek who was standing at the head of the line.

Shaking his hand but not getting a response to his question Win pulled the door wider and gestured them all in.

Sitting them in his living room he waited until they'd introduced themselves, triggering the memories that always floated at the surface.

The one case he'd never solved, that one, solitary outlander that had stayed with him. As they took turns bringing him up to date, he heard them out without comment.

Staring longest at Cleo he stroked his chin thoughtfully, he was an open-minded man, it was part of the reason why he had such a good solve rate in his day, but psychics?

He'd had a few come forward over the years, especially for the Gardner kid case, but he hadn't set much stock in what they'd said.

He'd even followed up on a few of the leads they'd given him, desperate for anything, he'd clutched every piece of information like a drowning man grabbing a life ring.

Of course, it hadn't come to anything, he hadn't really thought it would, but this one intrigued him.

Her direct, open gaze spoke of someone honest; she believed in what she was saying, he thought, she wasn't deliberately misleading a grieving family. That didn't mean she wasn't unintentionally doing so though.

Her hand was cool and soft in his when he shook it, for a brief moment she squeezed before letting go. Sitting back in the chair she spoke quietly, but directly to him.

"You don't believe me, but you trust me, an unusual combination."

Returning her gaze, he was just as direct.

"Clever party trick Miss Hart. Although you're right, I don't believe in psychics, but my copper's gut instinct tells me you aren't a con artist."

Andy jumped in, "She knows things, things that were never released at the time. I can't say I'm entirely sure about this psychic thing but I'm willing to do anything if it helps find out what happened to my sister."

"You do realise I'm retired, don't you? I'm not sure what help I can be."

Andy nodded, "I know. We're here to pick your brains, is there anything about the case you can tell us that might help? Why would Willow direct us to George Bellows only for us to find him dead?"

Win looked at him thoughtfully, seeing the face of the boy Andy was the night he'd met him.

Tiny, pinched face and eyes blurred with unshed tears as he tried to be brave.

The man he saw today still held that aura of a little boy lost, it surrounded him like a smell he couldn't wash away.

Win knew all too well what being trapped in the past did to a man, Willow's disappearance had shaped his life, and his career.

Plucking a cigarette from the pack on the table next to him Phelps lit up.

"I interviewed everyone personally, those three boys that were picking on you lot just before Willow went missing, and the woman who said she saw her heading to the toilet block on her own. I got no leads from any of them. My best guess was that while you lads were fighting Willow wandered off to use the loo, maybe someone saw her and intercepted her, someone who cut off her hair to disguise her. After that, the trail goes cold."

Stubbing out his cigarette Win got up without explanation, left the room, and then returned carrying a cardboard box which he placed in the middle of the floor.

"This is everything I have on the case. I copied it all before I retired, and once in a while I get it out and look through it in the hopes something new will come up."

Sweeping the puzzle pieces into a box he cleared the table and started laying it out with the contents of the box. Digging in a drawer he got out some blue tack which he used to put up photos on the wall.

"We need one of those whiteboards really, but this'll have to do for now."

The others crowded around the table and wall, only Andy hung back, the sight of his sister staring out at him in a photo from happier times made his stomach lurch.

Evan had already pulled out a chair and was flicking through one of the folders while Derek picked up another. Steve, who didn't seem comfortable with the retired detective just read over Evan's shoulder.

Cleo reached for a dark green, cardboard envelope, but as she flexed her fingers to grab it Win's voice stopped her.

"That's the crime scene photos, although we didn't find a body they're still upsetting."

Phelps glanced away for a moment as he thought of that pile of blonde curls and the smears of blood, the ripped, stained red shorts, and the stuffed rabbit of which there'd been no sign.

Cleo nodded but didn't put the envelope down, she slowly opened it and ran a finger across each image as though trying to touch it.

She closed her eyes, leveled her breathing, and focused.

A small, grubby face, streaked with tears, a misshapen stuffed rabbit in one hand, its eyes skew-whiff giving it a puzzled expression. The other hand stretched towards something or someone, but Cleo couldn't see who or what before it vanished.

Five questioning faces were looking at her when she opened her eyes, waiting to hear what she'd seen.

"Not a lot guys, sorry. I got the impression that she was reaching out to someone or something, maybe as DCI Phelps here said, someone intercepted her on her way to the toilet block."

"You can call me Win or Phelps, no need for the title, I'm retired. That said, I do still have a couple of contacts in the station, I'll get in touch with them, and see what I can find out about Mr. Bellows, and the manner of his death."

After they'd gone, he looked at the wall he'd created.

Willow's innocent little face in the middle, a photo of that Margo woman who'd seen her, the fairground lad, and the three boys who'd been roughhousing with Andy and his friends.

Getting another folder from the bottom of the box, one that he'd carefully kept to himself earlier, he read the list of known sex offenders who'd been living in the area at the time. Every one of them had been meticulously checked by his team and then double-checked by him personally, and all but two had an alibi for that night.

Arnold Green & Simon Cleverly.

Both had a history of inappropriate behaviour with children of around the age Willow had been at the time.

Arnold had used his position as a photographer's assistant to gain access to children.

Simon had been more impulsive, hanging around the local parks and swimming pools until he found a kid susceptible to his tried and tested offers to show them his new puppy. Amazing how the old methods still worked.

They hadn't been able to prove they weren't in the area, but Win hadn't been able to prove they had been either. He'd hauled them in for questioning of course, but he'd got nowhere. These had been his main leads, he'd long suspected one of them had something to do with Willow's disappearance, and the frustration of not being able to prove it had driven him mad. Staring at the mug shots of the two men he curled his lip in disgust.

Simon stared out at him with eyes as big as saucers, his round face looked childlike and innocent despite his long history of offending.

Arnold on the other hand looked more like your stereotypical pedophile.

His narrow, pointed face and close-set eyes created the face that you had in mind when you told your kids not to speak to strangers. Lank, greasy hair curled onto the collar of his nylon tracksuit top, and he scowled at the camera as though irritated at his arrest.

Win flicked the corner of the photo thoughtfully, he could feel a familiar buzz of adrenaline, the one he always felt when he was a detective.

It wouldn't hurt to pay the two men a visit and have a little chat, maybe with so much time gone by one of them would slip and tell him what he needed to know.

Chapter 7

Pulling up outside his mother's house, the same house he'd grown up in, Andy felt his stomach clench.

Cleo was sat silently in the passenger seat, he'd asked her to come along, his mother was more likely to open up to her than him. Before he'd left home a procession of psychics had visited her, each one happy to take her money before clutching at one of Willow's much-loved toys and feeding her a story.

The Jilly he'd known would welcome Cleo with the open arms she didn't hold out for her only living child.

She pulled the door open so quickly he guessed she'd been standing behind it watching them walk up the path.

Nothing had changed, the hall was a shrine to his sister, as was the living room. Every spare inch of wall space was taken up by blown-up photos of her through every moment of her short time with them.

The rest of the room was neat as a pin, he could smell the lingering odour of bleach, clogging his throat and stinging his eyes. Jilly was still cleaning fanatically, he thought sadly.

It was his enduring memory of her, spraying, scrubbing, wiping, and scouring at every surface. Her hair coming loose from the tight bun and curling around her face which was flushed from exertion.

Currently, the woman herself was unflushed, her hair scraped back from her lined face, her eyes clear but devoid of the sparkle that had once bought them to life.

Flicking a hand at the sofa she took the armchair after giving Andy a cursory hug with stiff arms.

He introduced Cleo, and as he'd thought, the light of interest glowed on his mum's face.

Jumping up from her seat she offered refreshments, Cleo followed his lead in politely refusing. They'd already agreed not to share everything but instead, to suggest that Cleo had "sensed" Willow, which would hopefully prompt his mum to talk but not raise her hopes too much.

Jilly leaned forward eagerly throughout Cleo's explanation, nodding regularly as if agreeing with everything she heard.

"Is there a message for me? Do you need something of hers to hold to get through to her?"

Cleo winced, she was more than aware of the charlatans that preyed on the vulnerable and grieving, and the tactics they used.

"No Mrs. Gardner, not yet. I just need to hear about her, everything you remember from when she went missing."

Andy saw the light of obsession burning even brighter, pulling out a box she started passing Cleo newspaper clippings. Each faded, yellowed sheet bore the same smiling photo of Willow.

"There were no leads, nothing. It was as though my girl just vanished into thin air."

Cleo scanned the articles, after the first one they were just a rehash of the same information, nothing new had come to light and the papers had used the trick of re-writing it and quoting "unnamed sources and experts."

She was just about to hand them back when she stopped and re-read the one at the bottom.

According to this, a local journalist had been told by an unnamed "police source" that locally known sex offenders were being checked out.

The writer had been careful not to name any of them, but Cleo wondered why this hadn't come up when they spoke to DCI Phelps earlier.

Handing the article to Andy she turned to Jilly.

"Is there anything you think was overlooked?"

Jilly nodded eagerly and produced a notebook which she flicked through until she got to the page she wanted.

"There was the local sex offenders' angle, plus no one followed up on the boy the fairground worker saw, that could've been Willow after her hair was cut off. What better way to smuggle her out than to pretend she's a boy."

For the first time, Jilly looked at her son.

"You tell her Andy, remember that clairvoyant that came to us? He said he could see Willow living as a boy. The police didn't take it seriously, another lead that just slipped by them."

Andy gave his mum a tight smile.

He remembered all too well.

The clairvoyant was a large, rotund man, sweating profusely into a hanky that he used to constantly mop his face. Clutching Willow's nightdress, he'd thrown back his head and let his eyes roll back. Telling Jilly, the story of "seeing Willow dressed as a boy and living in Scotland."

She'd hung off his every word, and after he'd shuffled his overstuffed self out of the house she hadn't let up until his dad had agreed to drive her to Scotland. They'd spent two weeks driving all over the country, showing Willow's photo to everyone they saw. Of course, no one had seen her, but it hadn't put Jilly off. She'd been straight on the phone to Phelps, nagging him to chase it up.

It was yet another milestone on Jilly's path to obsession.

Every time someone had given her so much as a sniff of a lead, a rumour, gossip, anything was enough to set her off.

Once his mum was sure that she'd had everything she could get from Cleo she started looking pointedly at the clock on the mantelpiece.

The MBNF group was due in forty minutes he realised.

Standing up he couldn't help but notice the look of relief on his mum's face that they were leaving.

Trying to hide his hurt he tried to give her a hug, she stepped back so just his hands ended up touching the tops of her arms. He leaned in and brushed a kiss on her wrinkled cheek.

Andy felt her tense, he knew she was trying not to pull away from him, swallowing the lump in his throat he set his face so she wouldn't see the hurt there.

No point anyway, the part of her that had loved and cared for him for the first ten years of his life, had died the night Willow had gone missing.

Phelps was sat at a table at the back of the pub.

One of those fast dying out, traditional ones it sported a darts board, pool table, and a dazzling array of real ales that the landlord personally felt proud of.

Far enough from the station Phelps knew he was unlikely to see any of his former colleagues here, and since he was meeting his connection, DS Stephanie Wright, it was better they didn't get seen together.

Steph had a glass of white wine which she'd quickly downed half of, the unspoken part of the deal being that Phelps got the drinks, and she was clearly going to be getting her money's worth.

"George Bellows, his report suggests suicide, but the DCI is suspicious about the state of the house. He could've turned it over himself before slitting his wrists, but it looks as though someone was looking for something. That other name you gave me, Frank Monroe, I ran him through the system, and nothing. Lives at the address he once shared with his mum before she passed away, no job, no arrests, nothing. We've had a couple of callouts to his address, locals giving him grief, that sort of thing. Arnold Green was recently released from custody after a recall for breaching the terms of his licence. Simon Cleverly has just about managed to skirt a custodial, lots of complaints but when we investigate it's hard to get evidence, and witnesses that'll make a statement."

Phelps gulped a mouthful of ale.

"Should be Luckily not Cleverly"

Steph snorted in agreement and nodded.

"We all know what he's up to, but he's streetwise enough to pick victims that won't want to make it official."

"What's DCI Brooks like?"

"He's good, not in your league of course, who is, but he's meticulous enough, and he won't back off from a case if he thinks there's more to it. The Bellows case is in safe hands if that's what you're asking."

Win grinned at her, "You know me so well dear Steph. Although not entirely, I was also wondering if he'd be open to talking to me."

Steph waggled a hand back and forth.

"Hmm, possibly. He does tend to think outside the box, but at the same time he won't put a case at risk, and he might see bringing you in as a risk."

Smiling back at her ex-boss she cocked her head to one side.

"I could test the waters though, see how the land lies."

When Phelps took a swig out of his glass to hide his smug smile, and she shook her head in mock dismay.

"You always did know how to get your own way boss."

Steph had one more name for him.

"I had a dig through the old files myself and ran a few of the other names to see if anything of interest came up. The only one that hit was Margo Granger, the woman who said she saw Willow heading to the toilets that night. She's become a self-made local celebrity who pushes herself forward into every re-hashed newspaper story on the case, or I should say was. Margo had a nasty fall down the stairs just before George was found dead, nothing suspicious, she'd been wearing high heels and it looks as though one caught in the carpet at the top of the stairs. We did a routine check on her calls, and one was in coming around the time it happened so assumably she was rushing to answer it when she fell, and then broke her neck at the bottom. I can't see any way it links but as you used to say, the devils in the detail."

Win took a mental note, as Steph said, it wasn't enough to raise suspicions, but he wasn't a man who ignored coincidences either.

Moving on to station gossip Phelps tried to feign interest in who was shagging who, and who was tipped for a promotion. He'd never been good with social niceties, but he genuinely liked Steph and didn't want her to feel as though he was all take and no give.

DS Wright, however, knew him only too well, the problem was, what else did she talk to Phelps about? He had no hobbies outside of work as far as she knew.

He got another round and listened to another forty minutes of gossip before deciding that he'd met his social skills quota for the day.

As he strolled back towards his bungalow, he ran the new information through his head, this case was back on his agenda and this time he was going to solve it.

Chapter 8

Cleo had taken herself off to bed early, Andy had dropped her off earlier before going off for some "time on his own." Clearly shaken by the visit to his old family home Cleo hadn't blamed him.

The others were sprawled around the lounge, and it looked as though they were planning a session, but Cleo wasn't in the mood for drinking or company.

She planned a soak in the bath with a book and then try to get a good night's sleep.

It felt as though things were heating up and she hadn't heard from Willow since they'd found George's body. It was possible that was all she'd wanted and had now gone, but Cleo had a strong feeling there was more to come.

Leaning back in the hot, foamy water, Cleo felt the tension drain away, her eyelids felt too heavy to keep open and she struggled to focus on the book she was reading. The words swam in front of her eyes, and she found herself reading the same paragraph two or three times.

Putting the book to one side she slid under the water until it framed her face, closing her eyes she felt more relaxed than she had since this all began.

Enjoying the pleasant feeling of drifting between sleep and wakefulness she listened to the sound of the water gurgling.

FRANK MONROE

Sitting up with a start she caused the water to slosh over the side of the bath.

THEY WILL PAY

The voice had been loud, and insistent, but sounded very much like Willow again. Pulling herself out of the tub she wrapped a large, fluffy towel around herself.

The voice had gone.

Pulling on a pair of baggy, faded, PJ bottoms and a T-shirt she leaned against the pillows, the bed was soft, and she felt as though she was falling into a cloud.

Her eyes fluttered, then closed.

His round, flabby face was pushed up close to hers.

Little piggy eyes, sunken into his flesh like raisins pushed into dough, her heart beat faster. Cleo held her breath and then released it slowly, hoping to calm herself.

The face pulled back and vanished from sight.

FIND FRANK

The words were an echo, as though coming from a great distance.

Cleo felt a sensation like falling into an abyss with the air rushing through her ears, but strangely, there was no sense of fear as she dropped into the unknown.

Find Frank, they will pay

This time the voice was quieter, barely above a whisper and Cleo had to strain to hear it.

The sense of falling sped up and this time her stomach lurched and turned over. She tried to reach out and find something she could grasp to stop herself, but her hands batted against the wind helplessly.

She screwed her eyes up tight and clenched her fists, waiting for the inevitable thump of a hard landing.

Cleo had awoken before hitting the ground.

Sitting up in bed she stared around the room, disorientated for a moment by the strange surroundings.

Remembering where she was, she took a moment to calm herself.

Tapping the screen of her phone she realised it was only 9 pm, not late at all. Downstairs the others would still be up and maybe Andy would be back too.

Deciding she needed to share her new message Cleo swung her legs out of bed and stuffed her feet into a pair of fluffy slippers. Pulling a hoodie over her T-shirt she decided the PJ bottoms would be fine, she really couldn't be bothered to change them.

In the lounge the group were all spread out across the chairs and sofas, clutching glasses and bottles of beer the conversation was a pleasant hum.

When they heard the door opening and saw Cleo the talking slowly stopped until she was faced with the awkward situation of a silent group now staring at her as though waiting for her to speak.

Deciding that she needed a drink Cleo helped herself to a glass of white wine before explaining why she was standing in front of them in her nightwear.

"Frank Monroe. That's the next message, I also saw a face this time, I think it was his."

Evan snorted, "Fat kid with small nasty eyes?"

Cleo nodded, "Yep that's the one. Did we ever find out where he was?"

Evan pulled out his phone and started scrolling through the contacts list.

"I know a man who might know, my editor, the one who called about Margo. He's been with the paper for donkey's years."

Standing up and pacing the room while he spoke Evan's voice became sharper, more like the one he used for his day job.

"Hi Neil, sorry to call so late. I'm trying to track down a bloke called Frank Monroe. I went to school with him, and I think there might a story there."

This was followed by Evan nodding and making Hmmm sounds, scrabbling for a pen and a sheet of paper he started scrawling some notes.

"Interesting Neil. Thanks for that, yeah, you get first dibs, always mate."

Hanging up he waved the paper in the air excitedly.

"Not much on him, he was interviewed for a story on the area where he lives, apparently it's gone to pot and he's one of the residents that attracts a lot of the youngster's anti-social behaviour."

Steve rubbed his face with his hand as though dry washing.

"I might be able to find someone who knows the local kids around there that can fill us in a bit more."

The group looked at Andy.

"We need our retired detective, and you seem to be the one he's more likely to help."

Looking at the clock Andy pointed out it was a bit late to be making calls to anyone.

"We'll have to pick this up again tomorrow."

Cleo had refilled her glass and found a spare seat; the conversation had returned to the relaxed murmur of old friends catching up, and she leaned back listening to the various voices.

She was so relaxed she hadn't noticed at first that Evan was watching her, his blue eyes fixed on her face, and she saw him blush as he realised, he'd been caught.

She gave herself a mental shake, there was no room in her life for a good-looking ladies' man, she told herself sternly.

Win pulled up outside the block of flats where Simon lived. Out of the two his MO of hanging around places where he'd find kids and impulsive behaviour fit Willow's disappearance more than Arnold's.

Cleft House loomed over the cracked concrete parking area, it should've been condemned years ago, thought Win. He'd spent most of his uniform years making arrests here, and it didn't look as though it had changed much.

As he got out of the car a small boy with a shaved head and wearing a grubby name-brand tracksuit shuffled over.

"I'll look after your motor for a tenner."

Win directed his police officer stare at the boy who shrugged.

"Discount for old bill. I'll do it for a fiver."

Phelps hid his smile, he'd always had a sneaky admiration for ingenuity, he rummaged in his pocket and pulled out a handful of coins and handed £2.50 to the boy.

"The rest if I come back and it's all in one piece."

The kid nodded and stuck the coins in his pocket before leaning himself against the car taking up "guard duty"

Pushing open the main door, the intercom system had been vandalised and the doors weren't locking anymore, and the smell of stale urine made him wince. Breathing through his mouth he cussed as he saw the sign that declared the lift out of use.

Luckily Simon lived on the second floor so not too many steps, it was more that repulsive smell that made his eyes water that he'd hoped to avoid by using the lift.

The stairwell was occupied at various points by young men and a few girls, they all wore the uniform of tracksuits and trainers, and all had the same hostile air about them.

Sharp eyes followed his progress and conversations stopped as he went by.

He picked up a few muttered "Pig" comments but being a man who chose his battles wisely he ignored them.

Simon's front door was swinging back and forth.

The fresh splinters of wood on the frame suggested that someone had smashed it through.

Win knocked, he heard light footsteps and then breathing on the other side as though the occupier was standing behind the door.

"Simon Cleverly? DCI Phelps."

Win knew he was potentially pushing his luck but had decided explanations could wait and he was best off just declaring himself to be police to start off with.

The door swung open just enough for Simon to look around and check his visitor, and seeing that it was indeed someone who smelt and looked like an officer allowed Win access.

Simon's face was still rounded, but the cherubic appearance of his younger days was gone.

Instead, his head looked like a round lolly on his stick-thin body, Simon's pasty skin looked as thin as paper, and his eyes were sunken back into the sockets, giving him a skull-like appearance that made Phelps shudder.

The hall was cluttered with stacks of old magazines and newspapers, the room smelt mouldy, and the dust was tickling Win's nose, he wriggled it in the hopes of stemming a sneeze. Following the man into another dust-mote-filled room, Win looked dubiously at the sofa he'd been invited to sit on.

It sagged on broken springs and was coated with what looked like animal hair, not that there was any other sign of a pet.

Simon was fidgeting uncomfortably with the buttons on his old-fashioned cardigan and avoiding looking Win in the face.

"Simon, I'm here about a historic case. Do you remember Willow Gardner going missing? I spoke to you at the time, and you couldn't confirm your whereabouts, if you could think back and give me a bit more information it would be helpful to eliminate you from our enquires."

Simon gulped, but a bit more colour came back to his face, he'd been expecting something else Win surmised.

"I remember her officer. I told you at the time I was up the shops getting some bits for my elderly mother."

"Simon, we didn't find you on any CCTV, and you couldn't produce a receipt or any evidence that you were there."

Simon sniffed and then wiped his nose on his sleeve, Win kept his face blank not wanting the man to see how much he disgusted him.

"My mum backed me up."

His voice had taken on a petulant whine, like a child demanding a pack of sweets.

"I'm sure she did Simon, but then in my experience, that's what mothers do. Would she still back you do you think?"

Simon's face took on a slightly smug expression

"Don't know officer, she passed away a few years ago, hence I'm living in this shithole where the other residents spray paint my door and regularly kick it in. You lot aren't interested then."

That explained why the door was half hanging off its hinges, Phelps guessed the locals had found out about Simon's past and were making their feelings felt.

Win nodded as though with sympathy but didn't comment.

"It was interesting though, looking at your history. You tend to be someone who likes to hang around where children play, and act impulsively if you spot one that's vulnerable."

He let it hang in the air, Simon fidgeted with a button again, pulling it out of the hole and pushing it back in over and over.

"I like boys, not girls."

The admission was spoken softly, almost as though Simon hadn't meant to say it.

"Someone cut off her hair, someone who maybe wanted her to look like a boy?"

Win put a question in his voice, guiding Simon to an answer that might corner him, but Simon stepped backward as though putting distance between the suggestion and himself.

"I. DID. NOT. TOUCH. THAT. KID."

The angry blush had spread over his face, Simon was making an angry denial, and much as it put him back to step one, Win had to admit he felt it was likely he was telling the truth.

Problem was, Phelps was pretty sure that Simon had done something with another kid, which was why he was focused on one denial rather than an overall "I didn't touch any kid."

He stood and walked back into the hall with Simon following him close behind, as they got to the door Win ran his hand down the frame. Swinging it back and forth, he made a point of how insecure it was.

"Looks as though your door needs fixing up Simon?"

Simon licked his dry lips and his eyes flittered nervously from side to side, Win smiled at him, before walking back out.

The stairwell might have been full of young gangbangers, but he felt less uncomfortable than he had in Simon's flat.

Tipping his head in a farewell he bounded down the stairs and with relief let himself back outside to where the lad was still propped on his car.

Digging in his pocket he ignored the change and pulled out a five-pound note.

The kid looked at it suspiciously, being offered a bonus obviously didn't happen in the world of car-watching very often.

"What can you tell me about the bloke on the second floor?"

The kid hungrily eyed the note.

"You mean the nonce? Likes to sit on the bench at the park and watch the little kids, a few of the parents kicked his door in and had a word."

Handing the prize over Win patted the kid's shoulder, he felt the fragile bones of someone who could do with a good meal, and then the way he flinched from being touched.

It made him feel sad, sad, and angry.

"My card's wrapped up in that note, if you need anything call. My name's Win."

The kid had got the card out and was scrutinising it

"Mine's Hopper."

Glancing around to make sure no one had seen him take a card from an obvious member of the constabulary, the kid darted off toward one of the blocks of flats.

Phelps watched him go, there'd been Hoppers at every estate he'd ever been to over the years.

Getting in his car Win drove away, without so much as a backward glance.

Chapter 9

Frank lumbered his huge weight across the room, opening the fridge he absently piled items on the table behind him.

A four-pack of chocolate puddings, a bar of chocolate, and the butter for spreading thickly across the toast he had cooking. He also took out a plastic bottle of cola and added it to the collection that made up the snack he was having as an after-dinner extra.

He'd already eaten a pack of bacon, four eggs, and six slices of toast for his tea, he didn't even think he was hungry, it was more habit and boredom.

Frank didn't go out much.

His shopping was delivered, as was anything else he needed, sometimes he went to the local shop for extras he'd run out of, but he preferred to use the online apps to get those dropped off where he could. He paid more, but it was worth it.

Anything was better than facing the outside world when he didn't need to, the stares, the nudges, and the comments just loud enough for him to hear.

It was bad enough that they hung around his house most days. Teenagers, all of them overconfident and loud. Pushing and shoving each other playfully, drinking out of cheap tins of cider and lager while they boasted about who they were copping off with.

As the alcohol took hold they'd turn to him, Fat Frank was one of the names they'd given him, and that was among the repeatable ones.

Easing himself onto the sofa, a deep gulley showed where he always positioned himself, he laid out his treats on the coffee table within easy reach.

Switching on the tele he flicked the channels looking for a program to watch, he finally found an old film that he remembered from a few years ago.

Propping himself up slightly so he could eat without choking, he got comfortable.

His mum had passed away last year, and he desperately missed her company, fetching him snacks, getting him a blanket, and watching the soaps together.

She'd talked about the characters as though they were real, interspersing her dialogue about what they'd got up to with complaints about the real people in their area. The miserable, bad-tempered woman that had taken over the corner shop, the man who let his dog piss against their wall, and the screaming kids two doors up.

Frank felt the tears clogging his throat, the grief was never far away, there were times he could even hear her voice as though it was right here, next to him.

He'd eaten the three slices of butter-dripping toast, sprinkling crumbs across the sofa he'd put his plate on the table and snapped off a chunk of chocolate.

As he felt the richness melting in his mouth it was as though it gave him peace of mind.

Dark, unhappy thoughts scattered as though caught by the wind, food gave him solace.

His eyes drifted closed, half listening to the film, cozy on the sofa with his stomach filled to bursting.

"Frank"

The voice was sharp, female, and a little familiar, it made him sit up with a start, the film was still playing in the background so he couldn't have been asleep long. Frank's heart beat a bit faster; his mouth was dry and gummy, picking up the cola he swigged from the bottle. The little gassy bubbles popped on his tongue, and the rush of sugar relaxed him.

It was thinking of his mum, he reassured himself, he'd been so desperate to hear her that he'd conjured up a voice. He pressed pause on the film, freezing an image of the leading lady screaming, her mouth open, her eyes wide and scared.

"Frank!"

This time the voice sounded annoyed, Frank looked around the room, the fear made him swallow hard. The lamps that had made it feel cosy when he'd turned them on earlier, now cast deep shadows and created dark corners.

Frank pulled the blanket higher as though the flimsy material would offer him protection against whoever was in his house shouting his name.

When the voice didn't come again, Frank's heart rate slowed, although his breathing was still ragged and loud in the silence. He sat, still as a statue, ears tuned to every sound, slowly letting the blanket drop as he felt more secure that it had been his imagination.

Frank swung his legs around and heaved himself into a sitting position.

The childish giggle sounded as though it was right next to his ear, he was sure he felt the warm tickle of breath and the sofa give as though someone small and slight was crouched by his side.

"What do you want? Who are you?"

His voice trembled; someone was in his house.

"You will all pay"

The voice hissed at him, still childish but with an underlying hatred that made his blood turn to ice.

Was it one of the kids? Was someone playing a prank on the local fat man, Frank licked his dry lips and fumbled for his phone. Better to call the police and potentially look foolish he thought.

Lighting up the screen, his finger poised to press the 9 three times, he nearly passed out when the phone was ripped from his hand. It bounced across the room into one of the dark, unlit corners where its screen created a blue glow.

Feeling suddenly vulnerable sitting down, Frank heaved himself to his feet, this took considerable effort. His weight dragged him back down as he pushed himself up on his hands. Another breath next to his other ear sent him tumbling back into his seat. His name was no more than an urgent whisper this time.

He felt his heart speed up again, he gave a sharp intake of breath at the jolt of pain.

Frank broke out in a cold sweat, his clammy hands' clutching at the blanket as though seeking comfort. The pressure in his chest was building, it felt as though someone had reached into his chest and was squeezing his heart in an iron grip.

It was hard to put his thoughts together now, he couldn't catch his breath, and Frank's chest hitched with the effort.

The pain stabbed under his ribs like a sharp blade, falling to his knees onto the dirty carpet he tried to focus on his mobile phone.

The screen went dark, unable to see it but sure of its approximate location he crawled like an uncoordinated baby across the floor.

Every movement bought a fresh wave of pain, his wrists and arms not strong enough to support his weight he collapsed forwards.

Frank forced himself to move.

Dragging himself towards the corner of the room on his forearms and pushing himself on with his knees. His nose touched the top of the carpet pile, it smelt stale and musty and the dust bunnies tickled his skin.

Groping with his right hand he finally felt the reassuring bulk of his phone under his fingers, and the screen lit up.

Pressing the button 3 times he heard the operator ask what service he required.

Unable to suck in any more air his arms folded under him as he tried to lift his head to speak.

Frank fell sharply to the right; he remained aware long enough to hear the dull thud as he hit the corner of the tv stand.

He could taste the metallic blood in his mouth as the hand around his heart gave one final hard squeeze, and he was sure he heard a light, girlish giggle.

DCI Brooks took in the scene in the living room.

The house was cluttered and dusty with an underlying stale smell that suggested it had been some time since it was last cleaned. Sprawled under the giant TV screen was the body of the grotesquely overweight householder, Frank Monroe.

His head was turned so it faced Brooks, the puddle of blood from the head wound soaking into the carpet.

An aborted 999 call had been traced to this address, and entry was forced when no one responded to paramedics and uniform officers knocking on the door. When the body was discovered the amount of blood and the disarray in the room had raised suspicions, any death deemed "unexpected or suspicious" meant a police investigation, so here he was, along with his DS, Steph Wright.

Leaving the men in white suits to do their business Brooks wandered back outside where a group of neighbours were watching the drama unfold. Eager faces peered over the shoulders of uniforms trying to see something exciting and phones were waved in the air as people recorded the action for their social media feeds.

Brooks narrowed his eyes and jerked his head to the nearest officer.

"Get rid of them. Now."

The officer, a young man who was eager to make a good impression on his senior nodded eagerly before striding off to the rubberneckers.

"Nothing to see people, get yourselves home."

There was nothing that irritated Brooks more than people who found the sight of death enthralling, today's world where images like these would be posted around the various networks within the hour dismayed him.

Many a case had ended up going awry because potential witnesses preferred to get their moment of online glory than help the police solve a crime.

Turning to Steph he gave a deep sigh of discontent, standing with his back to the crowd, no need to get himself on camera, he gestured towards the house.

"I'm thinking an accident, maybe a heart attack looking at the size of him. Three unexpected deaths in the same town in such a short timeframe are a bit unusual, but it's not as though there's anything to link them."

"Apart from two of them being mates as kids, and both being involved in the Willow Gardner case. Then there's the woman who was one of the last to see Willow before she vanished."

The voice belonged to retired DCI Win Phelps who'd appeared behind him. Phelps threw his butt on the floor and ground it with the heel of his shoe.

"DCI Phelps, as I live and breathe. How did you get yourself over here so quickly?"

Brooks shot a look at Steph; they'd once been thick as thieves, and he was in no doubt who'd been sharing information with the retired officer.

The look bounced off Steph like water off a duck's back, and she shrugged at him.

Win lit another cigarette, and after taking a long drag he blew the smoke towards the house.

"Willow's brother is back in town. All of the players are in one place for the first time in decades. Could be a coincidence I guess."

Brooks got the impression that Phelps didn't set much store in coincidences.

"I remember the case; I was a new uniform in those days but it's hard to forget a kiddie going missing. Might be worth my while having a chat with the brother, see if he can shed any light on why he's back in town."

Oliver watched Win's face as he spoke, trying to gauge a reaction, but the man kept his expression blank and didn't comment.

With a seemingly casual goodbye to both Steph and Oliver, Win gave the house one final long look before striding away.

Chapter 10

Cleo had a fitful night's sleep; a strange nightmare had woken her up in the early hours of the morning.

She couldn't remember the details, but she was left with the impression of a screaming blonde woman and the feeling of falling.

It didn't make much sense to her, but then sometimes she wondered what did considering the messages she got.

Downstairs the rest of the group sat around the dining table, the atmosphere heavy and silent. Andy was pushing scrambled eggs around his plate with his fork, Evan had only a cup of coffee in front of him, and Derek was just staring at his food as though waiting for it to bite him.

Only Steve was shoveling his breakfast in his mouth with the fervour of a starving man.

Unsure of what had cast a pallor over the day already, but hearing her stomach rumble, Cleo grabbed herself some eggs and toast.

Everyone muttered a good morning in her direction as she sat down, Evan managed a warm smile, but the rest were determinedly gloomy.

"DCI Phelps called first thing; Frank Monroe was found dead at his house last night. He's also told us that the woman who reported seeing Willow heading to the toilets that night has died fell down the stairs and broke her neck."

Andy waved his phone as though she needed the imagery of it to back up what he'd said.

Cleo couldn't answer him, she'd just forked in a huge mouthful of scrambled egg and toast, so she chewed impatiently and waited for him to expand.

"The police reckon Frank had a heart attack and smacked his head while trying to get to his phone. It could be nothing, but as Phelps said, it's a big coincidence."

Swallowing her mouthful Cleo washed it down with a swig of fresh orange juice.

"Since we all got here each name you get ends up dead, it has to be linked."

"I think the dream I had last night was Margo, a blonde woman?"

When Andy nodded, she sighed.

"I could see a screaming blonde woman and got the sensation of falling, but it was very disjointed."

Everyone was silent for a moment taking that in and it was Evan who spoke first.

"Phelps is on his way over here, he reckons the DCI that's investigating, Brooks, will want to speak to us as well."

Just then Reynolds appeared in the doorway followed by Phelps, his look of barely concealed annoyance at having a meal interrupted tickled Andy who ducked his head to hide his grin from the others.

Derek waved his arm at the hot plates loaded with food.

"Help yourself, officer. Plenty to go around."

Win eyed the food hungrily before heading over to pick up a plate from the warmer, he loaded it with bacon, eggs, toast, and mushrooms before smothering the food with a healthy amount of brown sauce.

"Talk among yourselves while I get this lot down me, it's been a while since anyone made me a decent breakfast and I intend to enjoy it."

He wasn't kidding either, head down he matched Steve for speed of consumption.

It wasn't long before he leaned back in his chair, he patted his stomach and released a loud belch.

"So, we appear to have a number of deaths that while they don't initially seem linked, all relate to Willow's missing person's case 30 years ago. We've also got our Cleo here, claiming she gets messages. Each name she's given us has then ended up dead."

Turning his eye on her he managed a wry grin.

"Let me know if my name comes up so I've got time to put my affairs in order."

The off-color joke lightened the atmosphere, and even Andy found himself chuckling at Win's dark humour.

"As it stands, these lads were part of a group of three that hung out at school together and were picking on you guys when Willow went missing. They were spoken to at the time, and I've had a read through my notes to jog my failing, old man memory. All that told me, is that while they were obnoxious little shits, they didn't twang my radar as potential suspects. I'm now wondering if I wrote them off too quickly, did they know something that they didn't share with me at the time?"

"So, where do we start?"

Derek looked brighter than he had earlier, the input from the detective seemed to have revitalised him.

"I say we have a chat with Terry Peck. He's one of the last of the boys left, maybe he'll feel anxious enough to share what he knows."

It was a Saturday, and with no school, they decided to just show up at Terry's house and hope his welcome was warmer than it used to be.

He lived in a large, detached house built on the outskirts of town where there used to be just scrubland. It was one of those red-brick homes that look exactly like everyone else's, with mock Tudor windows and a neatly mown lawn.

Steve hung at the back of the group looking uncomfortably over his shoulder as though waiting for someone to grab him and tell him to get back where he belonged.

Andy dropped back as well and matched his pace to Steve's, the least he could do is try and stand with him, he thought.

It was Win who marched confidently up the paved pathway and pressed the doorbell before standing back slightly and staring at the door.

After a short wait that felt like forever to the group, the door swung open and a tall, slim, woman stood on the step. Her brown hair was tied back in what seemed to be known as a messy bun and she was wearing a set of tight-fitting lycra.

From her flushed face and breathless welcome, they deduced she'd been exercising.

Sticking out his hand in greeting, Win introduced himself as a former police detective and asked if Terry was home.

The attractive woman shook her head.

"Sorry guys, Terry's at football practice. He plays for the local pub team, The Swan, they meet every Saturday morning at the pitch. It's probably more about the drinks afterward though."

She wiped her head on her arm and then flapped her hand in front of her face.

"If that's all I need to get back to my exercise DVD."

Win thanked her for her time and turned away as she closed the door.

"I know where they practice"

This was from Evan, and everyone turned to him in surprise.

"What's with the shocked faces? I used to play with them myself, how do you think I keep myself so fit and trim?"

Giving an exaggerated twirl and flexing his arms as though demonstrating his muscles, he grinned at the group.

"Come on you bunch of arses, let's get going, we haven't got all day."

This came from Win who was rolling his eyes at Evan's little show.

When they got to the large, green playing field near the pub they could see that the team was still in the middle of a 5-a-side practice match.

It seemed to consist of a very mixed bunch of players, while a few were fairly athletic, most were constantly stopping, hands on hips, bent over trying to suck in a few breaths from the exertion.

Terry was instantly recognisable, his lanky figure dashing up and down the pitch as he shouted instructions to the other men. Spotting an opportunity to get the ball Terry legged it straight at a pudgy guy in too-tight shorts and an ill-fitting T-shirt.

Sticking his foot out he caught the other player with his studs sending him crashing to the ground where he rolled about clutching his ankle.

Terry appeared unconcerned and dribbled the ball to the other end of the pitch where he expertly scored a goal.

His celebrations were a bit one-sided, as most of the team had already run up to the injured player and were trying to help him to his feet.

A short, stocky man, with buzz-cut grey hair, stomped over to Terry, from the look on his face he was trying to remonstrate with him about the dodgy tackle, but it was clear that Terry wasn't at all concerned.

Shrugging the other man off he bounced on the spot as though eager to get at it again, but despite Terry's enthusiasm for continuing the others had clearly had enough as they started to straggle off the pitch.

Andy noticed that Terry walked back to the changing rooms alone, the other men appeared to be steering clear of him. Interesting, thought Andy, looks as though Terry is as popular now as he was back then.

The group followed behind and then hung around waiting outside the block until their target came out. Derek approached him first, his hand held out and introducing himself and then the others.

"Do you remember us? You must remember Andy; he was the kid whose little sister went missing at the fair."

Terry narrowed his eyes and then glared at them.

"It's not as though we were mates, was it? What do you want with me now?"

Evan moved forward and took that one.

"Might be best off doing this over a pint, you usually have one after the match don't you?"

Terry glanced around him as though wondering if he could slip away, the other players, now in their civies, were all heading towards the pub.

At the back of the group was the man Terry had tackled, an arm around each of his mates he limped towards the pub shooting Terry the bog eye as he went past.

Terry snorted, "If they aren't fit enough to play properly, they should hang up their boots."

Andy refrained from pointing out that however fit you were, a stud to the ankle was going to be a game changer.

The pub was humming with lunchtime customers, apart from the football team, there was another group playing a lively game of darts and a few families and couples eating lunch.

It took a while to find an empty table that wasn't too close to anyone else, Derek had gone to the bar, insisting that he get the first round in. Terry eyed them suspiciously, but his misgivings didn't stop him from taking the pint that Derek bought over.

"What do you bunch of outsiders want with me then?"

Andy almost smiled; it was strange, but at the same time comfortably familiar, to be called by their old nickname.

"We need to talk to you about George and Frank, have you heard what happened to them?"

Terry shrugged and gulped down a few mouthfuls of his pint, he wiped his mouth on the back of his hand before replying.

"I know about George, he worked at the school with me, but not Frank. I haven't seen him in donkey's years."

Win leaned in as though imparting a secret

"Frank was found dead last night. Out of the three of you, there's only you left."

Win left that part hanging in the air where it floated like a heavy black cloud.

For the first time, Terry looked uncomfortable, he shifted in his chair studying his pint as though the answer was at the bottom of the golden liquid.

"Still don't see what that's got to do with me."

The confidence had gone out of his voice, but the bluster remained.

"I'm not a big believer in coincidence Terry, what about you?"

The other man looked down at the tabletop, suddenly finding the damp ring from his pint glass fascinating enough to stare at.

Win continued as though Terry had answered him

"Maybe I could help, you know, get to the bottom of it, but I'd have to know what was going on. Any suggestions Terry?"

"No idea."

Terry swallowed the last of his pint and slammed the empty glass back onto the table, before standing up and pulling on his jacket.

"Gotta go, I'd like to say it was a pleasure to see you all again, but if I did, I'd be lying."

They all watched him storm out of the pub, flinging open the door with such force that it flapped in the wind for a while after he'd gone.

Chapter 11

Terry was still agitated when he got home.

His bad mood wasn't improved when he found his wife leaping around the living room in her lycra with the music blaring at full volume.

"Turn that shit off."

Rachel jumped, unfortunately, she'd been in the middle of a leg thrust so the surprise he gave her made her slip and land on her arse.

"For fucks sake Terry."

Her whiny voice irritated him, he punched the stop button on the handset and silence descended on the room.

Spinning on his heel he marched into the kitchen, threw open the fridge, and pulled out a bottle of lager. He waited until his wife came into the room before making a show of popping the cap using the worktop, he knew it wound her up and he was spoiling for a fight.

"You'll chip the worktop, Terry, honestly, you know how much that cost us."

So predictable his wife, it was always easy to get a rise out of her.

Rachel reached into the cupboard and got down a glass which she placed next to him.

He ignored it and drank straight from the bottle, something else that he knew would get on her wick.

"I don't know what's wrong with you today, it's like you want to wind me up."

"There's nothing wrong with me, I just don't see why I have to come home to you jumping around the house and the music blaring."

Rachel scowled at him; it wasn't worth trying to reason with him when he got like this, so she didn't bother.

"I'm going for a shower"

She flounced out of the room, and he heard the door slam before her footsteps pounded up the stairs.

He cracked open another bottle before he'd even finished the first, the pint at the pub earlier had given him a taste for it.

His urge for a drink hadn't been helped by that nosy retired copper and those waste-of-space outsiders.

No one had bothered to introduce him to the only woman at the table, nice looking bit of stuff, he thought, not sure what she was doing with those losers.

Terry drained the bottle and reached for the new one, but just as his fingers were about to brush the cold glass it skittered across the table and smashed to the floor.

The glass flew to all four corners of the kitchen, beer splashed across the floor, and all up the cabinets. He frowned, he hadn't touched it, yet it looked as though a malicious hand had shoved it to the floor.

He shook his head at his imagination, he must have caught it with the end of his fingers and not realised.

Now he'd have to clear it up, Terry fetched the dustpan and brush from under the sink and started sweeping the glass into it.

Shards had gone everywhere, large and small pieces glinted at him from the beer puddle, he huffed, why couldn't a man just sit with a cold beer and relax without some shit going wrong.

Terry stomped over to the bin and upended the dustpan emptying the glass into it, swiping up the mop bucket he dumped it in the sink and turned on the hot tap.

He gave it a squirt of floor cleaner before angrily slamming it on the floor slopping water over the sides.

He grabbed the mop and dunked it in, but as he stepped towards it to squeeze it out, he gave a shout.

Lifting his foot and twisting it to one side he could see a large shard of brown glass stuck in the sole.

He winced as he tugged it out, and blood stained the bottom of his sock.

Throwing the red-smeared glass into the bin with the rest of it he tried to ignore the feeling of discomfort worming through his stomach.

Cleo curled her legs up under her.

She was sitting on the bed at Derek's house trying to focus her thoughts, she'd heard nothing more from Willow since Freddie and Margo died.

Part of her didn't want any more contact, the part that was afraid that the next name would show up dead too.

The other part desperately wanted to hear from her, just so she could help Andy find out the truth.

It was hard to imagine how he'd managed to live with this for the last three decades.

Cleo closed her eyes and tried to empty her mind of static, but still, nothing came through.

She frowned; she'd never known a day when someone didn't attempt to make contact when she tried like this.

Unfurling herself from the bed she decided to take a wander downstairs and find out what the others were up to.

They were all in the living room, drinks in hand, listening to the retired police detective as he talked them through the case.

"Taken on their own each death looks accidental or unrelated, yet put together, they all have a clear link with Willow's disappearance."

Win's eye fell on Cleo at this point, she squirmed uncomfortably in the chair she'd plonked herself in.

"The only person that can tell us more is Willow herself. I feel a bit weird saying this, but are there any more messages that can help us, Cleo?"

This was it then, Cleo thought, the moment she had to admit she was getting exactly zilch and no help to anyone.

"Nothing. Not a bean. Nothing from Willow and nothing from anyone else which is also odd. Maybe she's given us all she can?"

Cleo noticed that Andy's shoulders slumped in disappointment and felt a stab of guilt, she so wished she could give him more.

Win shook his head, "That doesn't mean we're giving up. I've lived with this case being unsolved for too long, and if that's hard for me then it must be unbearable for Andy and his family. Although Terry didn't give us anything earlier his behaviour was interesting, that's a man who's hiding something and I intend to find out what it is."

He looked lost in thought for a moment as his mind wandered back to the original interviews he'd done.

Although he hadn't noted it in the official file, he clearly remembered being creeped out by a young Terry Peck.

The thought that he was now the headmaster of the local school with access to all those young minds wasn't computing either.

All those sick scenarios he'd come up with when Win had interviewed him had stuck in his head for years afterward. Pictures of poor Willow, torn limb from limb and being discovered in a shallow grave took root and haunted him day and night.

He'd give anything to solve this case, maybe then the nightmares would finally stop.

Jilly Gardner carefully polished the glass surface of the photo in a frame.

Willow's little face smiled out at her, forever five years old. She didn't have a photographic display of her daughter's journey into adulthood.

No cherished memories of her as a gawky, awkward teenager or starting her first job. Willow had never passed her driving test, she'd never see her fall in love, settle down, or have children of her own.

This was Jilly's daily ritual; each photo was lovingly cleaned and polished so she could always clearly see her beautiful daughter wherever she looked.

There wasn't a single photo displayed that didn't have Willow in it, the only ones that contained her ex-husband or her son always featured her daughter.

Andy had sent her numerous photos of his own daughter, and each one had been like a knife in her heart.

She'd stopped looking at them now, when the envelopes showed up and she could tell they contained photos she threw them in a drawer unopened. She wasn't able to toss them in the bin, but she couldn't bear to see them either.

Lissy.

Her only grandchild, and the spit and image of her Aunty Willow.

How Willow would have loved being an aunt, even at such a tender age Jilly could see what a kind, caring woman she would grow into. Now her niece was older than Willow was when she'd gone missing, and every year older she became would remind Jilly all the more of what she'd lost.

She knew how everyone saw her, a figure of pity that they strove to avoid in case her misfortune rubbed off on them. Other parents would hold their children closer and thank goodness that it was her and not them.

The grief that had turned to obsession had driven away first her husband, and then her son, her only living child.

She wished she could feel something for them, but the only love left in her heart was for the child who was no longer with her.

Andy had grown into a fine man.

She could see that, and she could even feel pleased about who he was, but she couldn't bring herself to love him as a mother should love her son.

It hurt him, she saw the pain in his face, heard it in his voice as she turned her back on his daughter, and she wished she could change how she felt.

Jilly had tried, the first time she'd gone to see a counselor her ex-husband had arranged it.

This was his last-ditch attempt to save their failing marriage, he hadn't put it like that, but she'd known.

Just as she'd known the moment he started his affair, not that she cared, but she was no one's fool.

The counselor had tried an older woman with a no-nonsense, but kind, approach that had probably worked with all of her other clients. Jilly had shown up each week, precisely on time. She'd sat through the attempts to "open up about her feelings" and to "Talk about Willow" until she thought she was going to scream. Eventually, came the last session, the one where the woman had suggested that Jilly "wasn't ready for this level of therapy." A nicely packaged collection of words that sounded better than "I'm sick of wasting my time on you."

She'd tried the group approach, her and Mark sat with all the other bereaved parents, sipping endless cups of tea while they took turns sharing the intimate details of their losses.

That had been short-lived, Jilly had point-blank refused to continue going, what was the point of it, she'd asked.

Their daughter was missing, all these other parents had closure, and they knew what had happened to their child.

Taken by cancer, killed in a tragic accident, or stillborn, it was no less awful but not the same as their loss at all.

When Mark had carried on going without her, she'd been annoyed. How did he manage to find solace so easily when she couldn't?

It turned out he'd met someone, and the group was simply a way to cover for his extra-marital activities.

Jilly had thought she'd be hurt, upset, and jealous, but that was the her from before.

The new Jilly didn't care a less, and that was the death toll for her marriage.

Mark, thinking that this might be a catalyst to clearing the air, was in for a terrible shock when his wife of 15 years just shrugged at his confession. He dramatically announced he was leaving her, and she responded by helping him get his things together.

All she asked for was that she kept the house, the home where they'd been a family was now a shrine to all she'd lost.

It was also her prison.

Shackled to the house, waiting and watching for a day when her Willow came back to her.

Jilly picked up the next photo, it was the largest one with an ornate silver frame.

This was one of her favourites, taken only a couple of weeks before she disappeared.

In it, Willow was in her mother's arms, with her little elfin face pressed against her mum's cheek.

Every time she looked at it, she was transported to that day, the weight of her daughter's body, the softness of her skin against hers, and the feel of those little arms wrapped around her neck.

The blame she threw at others was only because of the weight of guilt she felt herself.

That night was her fault.

When Mark had suggested that Andy take Willow for a while so they could enjoy themselves, she should have said no.

At ten years old, he was far too young for taking care of his little sister on his own, but Mark had insisted, and as usual, got his own way.

Jilly had seen it etched on his face and felt his pain every time she threw it at him.

She saw the guilt running through her son like poison in his blood, but she felt powerless to help him. The saying, "misery loves company" was so true, seeing them miserable, guilty, and in pain, had justified her own feelings. Understanding it was one thing, but changing it was beyond her.

Jilly placed the photo carefully back into place, it lived in the middle of the mantlepiece under a large mirror on what would've been the chimney breast wall when the house had an open fire years ago.

Glancing at the mirror she barely recognised the woman she'd become.

Lines scored her once smooth skin, and her mouth was turned down in a constant expression of unhappiness.

Her hair used to be dark and soft, but now it was mostly grey and coarse.

She was about to turn away, both from her reflection and from the thoughts it evoked when a movement caught her eye.

The temperature had dropped suddenly, and the whole room felt like a freezer.

The mirror had iced over, and she stared in fascination at the thin layer of cold water across its surface.

Suddenly her image was softer, blurred by the ice, and partly hidden behind the words that had been scrawled across the mirror.

"Not his fault"

Jilly blinked, but it was still there when she opened her eyes.

"Willow?"

The hope she could hear in her voice bought a lump to her throat, was this really her daughter?

As the temperature lifted and the ice started to melt, the words faded until they were just smears on the otherwise shiny mirror surface.

Chapter 12

Elizabeth Peck had aged with dignity, her back was ramrod straight, and her chin held high.

The lines on her face were deeper, and more seemed to appear almost every day, but Elizabeth was a believer that you made the most of what you had.

Each morning she'd carefully apply her day make-up, she'd style her hair, and choose an outfit that she felt befitted her age and flattered her still slender size.

Unlike her husband, she thought ungraciously, as she watched him slurp his cup of tea.

Arthur Peck's face was weatherbeaten, he spent as much time as he could out on the lakes carp fishing. He also liked to live in his "fishing clothes."

These were mostly camouflage-coloured, elastic-waisted items, and no matter how often she washed them there was always a faint, lingering aroma of fishiness about them.

Elizabeth sipped her own tea and tried not to wince at the noise he was making with his.

It was the same when he ate, he'd breathe around his mouthful of food, creating a horrible gushing, chomping noise that turned her stomach.

If she was honest, everything about Arthur irritated her, if it wasn't for the thought of the shame of a failed marriage, she'd have left him years ago.

Putting her cup in the sink ready to wash when Arthur's had joined it, she started preparing the vegetables for lunch.

Terry and his awful wife were due over, and she always did him a lovely home-cooked roast on a Sunday.

The apple of her eye, the light of her life, her darling son. The only thing that Arthur had done right in all the years of marriage was to give her Terry.

She cringed as she heard Arthur slam his mug in the sink, she swore he let it drop on purpose knowing how much it annoyed her. Elizabeth shot him a raised eyebrow look but didn't bother saying anything. It was pointless trying to talk to him about his bad habits, he just shrugged it off, and if anything did it all the more.

The oven was almost at the right temperature, a couple more minutes and she'd put in the apple pie she'd made for their pudding, Terry loved her apple pie with custard.

"Do you have to do that now?"

Arthur had just got out his fishing tackle box and was busy making something he called "rigs," which seemed to involve spreading twine and small weights all over the table she'd just cleaned down.

He gave her his usual response, a shrug, before continuing with what he was doing.

Elizabeth huffed in exasperation and turned her back on him, bending over she opened the oven door and then lifted the apple pie so she could slide it onto the shelf.

As she reached inside what felt like a cold hand gripped her forearm and pushed upwards, hard. She let out a scream as her flesh touched the hot shelf, trying to pull away she found she was being held in place by something invisible.

By this time Arthur had managed to tear himself away from his fishing activity and had appeared behind her

"Why are you holding your arm on that burning shelf, Liz?"

Elizabeth let out a howl of pain.

"I'm not, I can't get my arm off it"

Arthur frowned and covered his hand with a tea towel before reaching in to try and pull her out.

As soon as he touched her arm the invisible hand let go and she was able to pull away.

The shock had made her drop the pie so there was raw pastry and stewed apple all over the floor.

Stepping back quickly in case she got burned again Elizabeth felt her foot slide through the mess.

She fought to stay upright but couldn't get a grip.

After a second of struggle her foot went from under her and she came crashing to the floor landing hard on her side.

When she heard a loud crack, she knew she'd broken something, then the pain flashed behind her eyes.

As she passed out, she swore she heard the tinkle of a childish laugh.

The day had been spent rehashing everything they knew, or thought they knew, about Willow's disappearance and how that might link to the recent deaths.

They hadn't even stopped to eat; Reynolds had bought some sandwiches and they'd stuffed them down without pausing in their task. It hadn't got them anywhere though, all they had was a list of deaths.

"My mum mentioned known sex offenders who were local to the fair. Did you look into all of them?"

Win had been hoping to keep that angle away from the group, with the usual responses to sex offenders it wouldn't take much for someone to go vigilante.

"It was one of the first things I did, but we couldn't find any evidence that any of them had even been near the fair that night."

Disappointment flashed across Andy's face; Phelps knew he'd pinned his hopes on that being another lead.

He felt bad about hiding the two suspects on his list but didn't feel it was something he should share unless anything came of it.

He still had Arnold Green to speak to yet, and if anything came of it he'd consider sharing it with the group.

Win kept on the track that Terry was the key to the whole thing.

"My gut is shouting so loud I'm surprised none of you can hear it."

Derek had chuckled and couldn't help but add a witty comeback

"I don't think we could hear it over you digesting that massive breakfast you ate earlier."

The retired police officer had managed a small smile in his direction

"Okay, funny lad."

They'd all read the files a hundred times over, but by now the words were swimming into each other and no one was picking up anything new.

Andy sighed and pushed the folder away.

"The only thing I can think of is that they saw something and didn't tell us at the time."

Win nodded, "That's the most logical answer. Looking back, they were all difficult to interview, belligerent, rude, unhelpful, and in the case of Terry downright weird."

He tapped his chin with his finger thoughtfully

"The question now, is what did they see, and why didn't they tell me at the time?"

Andy muffled a yawn with his hand, although they hadn't done anything strenuous, he was feeling as tired as if he'd run a whole marathon, Derek saw him and smiled.

"Maybe we should leave it there and try and get some sleep? Start fresh in the morning, see if stepping back gives us some new insight into it all."

The room agreed and Win started packing up.

"I'm going to leave all of this here tonight, saves lugging it over in the morning."

As soon as the door had closed behind him the others were saying their goodnights and heading up to their respective rooms.

Andy laid back on the pillows, despite the exhaustion he'd felt earlier he was struggling to get off to sleep now.

He closed his eyes and his thoughts wandered to his little sister.

Was she dead?

All the evidence seemed to suggest she was, how else would she be making contact with Cleo?

It all ran around his head, swirling ideas and theories bubbling out of the fog of weariness until finally, he fell asleep.

She was standing there, hands on her hips, just like she did when she was stubbornly refusing to pick up her toys or didn't want to go to bed.

113

Willow was unchanged, her little pointed face was turned up towards him, mouth set and eyes staring in an expression of stubbornness.

"Hey Wills"

His voice sounded as it had when he was ten years old, but somehow that felt as though it was exactly as it should be.

"You don't listen, Andy!"

Her cross little voice echoed through time and warmed his heart, how he'd longed to hear it one more time.

"I always listen to you Wills"

Willow stamped an impatient foot and shook her head making her blonde curls bounce.

"No, you don't! None of you listen to me!"

Andy tried to move towards her, his arms were already outstretched ready to hug her close, but no matter how hard he tried he didn't shift an inch.

"Its portant Andy. Very portant."

Willow's face creased up, the way it did when she was trying not to cry, it broke his heart not to be able to go to her.

"Find me Andy. I's lost."

Waking with a start he took a moment to orientate himself.

The dream was still vividly real, and his arms ached to hold his little sister again.

Andy put his hand up to his face, his cheeks were damp with tears.

Swinging his legs out of bed he jammed his feet into his slippers, no time for sleeping, he had to get on with hunting for the truth behind what had happened to his sister.

Terry paced up and down outside the hospital.

His mum had broken her arm in two places, and they were keeping her in overnight for observation.

She'd tearfully told him what had happened, and while he was sceptical about the idea that something had held her arm against the burning shelf, he was also starting to wonder if someone was digging into the past.

Someone who could find out his secrets.

If it was anyone, it was that retired detective, he'd been shocked to see him with the outsiders. He remembered when he'd interviewed him and the look of disgust on his face that he couldn't hide.

Terry stopped pacing, and a small, cold smile slid across his face.

He needed to know what was going on and what they knew, and the best way to do that was to see for himself.

He knew where Win lived, and that he lived alone, he'd break in tonight and take a look around.

An old man like that wouldn't be any challenge even if he did catch him.

All it would take would be an "accidental fall" like the one his mum had, maybe a slip down the stairs ending in a broken neck like that Margo woman.

That would do it, put an end to all of this poking about so he could get on with his life without constantly looking over his shoulder.

Decision made Terry jangled his keys and called over to his wife.

"Come on love, let's get ourselves off, they'll call if they need us to come back."

Rachel narrowed her eyes, her husband looked in an unusually good mood.

Considering his beloved mother was in the hospital, she wondered what had given him the spring in his step, and the nasty smug smile he was wearing.

Chapter 13

It hadn't taken much to wake up the others.

They'd all hastily dressed and rushed downstairs; Andy was pacing up and down. He started waving the list of witnesses at them as soon as they got through the door.

"The fair. We need to go to the fair, maybe that bloke Jay still works there, and besides we haven't even tried to look in the last place she was seen."

The group exchanged a look that wasn't lost on Andy

"The cheese hasn't slipped off my cracker so you can stop with that look."

Everyone shrugged, Derek picked up his keys and tossed Andy's to him

"Come on losers, let's get a shift on."

Andy felt a flood of warmth towards the little nerdy man who'd never once let him down in all the years they'd been mates.

It was as though Derek had read his mind when he stopped and patted his shoulder as he walked by. It was all he needed to know, that the outsiders would stand behind him, no matter what.

After leaving the group Win decided to try the other known sex offender on his list, Arnold Green.

Green lived with this mother in her neat-looking bungalow, the dim glow of the streetlamps lit up the outskirts of the playpark opposite. Win shook his head in annoyance, did no one check these things anymore?

Marching up the path he gave a sharp knock on the front door, the muffled sounds of the tele in the background reached him so he knew someone was home.

Eventually, the door swung open and a small woman in curlers and a dressing gown stood impatiently on the doorstep.

"DCI Phelps. Is Arnold home?"

Mrs. Green's shoulders slumped dejectedly as she nodded in response.

"Bit late for you to be dropping round, isn't it?"

Phelps didn't bother replying, he could tell she was already resigned to the police showing up when they wanted. When your son was a sex offender it became part and parcel of your life.

He squeezed by her into the small hall, the sound of the tele was coming from a room further down the corridor, but that wasn't where she pointed.

"Arnie is right here; he likes to be at the front of the house, so we moved the living room further back. It took a bit of getting used to, but he was right, it's much quieter down there for me. He's a good boy to his mother, taking the noisier front room so I can watch my programs in peace."

Win already had a good idea why Arnold preferred the front room, and it certainly wasn't so his mum could have some peace and quiet.

"I'll let myself in Mrs. Green, you go back to your programs."

Mrs. Green shot him an anxious look, twisting her hands nervously she flicked her eyes at the closed door.

"He doesn't like unexpected visitors; he won't be happy with me."

Phelps shrugged, "He must be used to unannounced visits by now though."

Arnold's mum shook her head, "We haven't had one for ages, I think we thought all of this was over now."

Win hid his frustration, the man was still on the register, and he should be getting his regular check-up visits. He'd drop a word with Steph, he decided.

Turning his back on the woman hovering behind him he pushed open the door without knocking.

Arnold was laying on the big double bed in just his underpants, the room was squalid, and Phelps winced at the sour smell of body odour and stale food.

He noticed Arnold hastily tucked something under his pillow when he saw he had a visitor before sitting up and pulling a sheet over his lower body.

Win shut the door in Mrs. Green's face and then strode into the room announcing he was from the police.

He didn't mention the retired bit, and Arnold didn't ask to see his ID, he was far too busy protesting at the sudden intrusion. He'd cut his long, greasy locks short. It looked like a home cut, and tufts of hair stuck out like gelled spikes.

His small, dark eyes darted around the room as though trying to see it from the police officer's perspective and work out how much trouble he was in.

Win strolled over to the far side of the room; it was the only area that was uncluttered apart from the professional-looking camera on a tripod set up.

The camera faced the window, and even though the curtains were now closed Win knew from the layout that when open Arnold would have a clear, unobstructed view of the park.

Which was exactly why he'd demanded this room.

Seeing what he was looking at Arnold immediately went on the defensive.

"I used to be a photographer until you lot destroyed my life. I still do it as a hobby though."

Win ran his finger down the camera and was pleased to see how irritated Arnold was by someone touching his possessions.

"If someone was to take a closer look at this camera, what photos would they find Arnold? Would there be anything on there that breaches the terms of your registration?"

The ferret-faced man blanched; he flicked out his tongue to wet his dry lips but didn't reply.

"We've re-opened a cold case, Arnold, remember Willow Gardner? You're still a person of interest, anything new to tell me?"

Arnold shook his head violently, "Nothing to tell officer. I never saw the kid; I didn't even go near the fair that night."

Phelps shook his head as though disappointed

"Tut, tut Arnold, I know you were there. I bet there are still photos to be found, photos of all the kiddies enjoying the rides."

He saw Arnold flash a glance toward the drawers in the corner of the room, Win took note of it for later use.

"I didn't touch any kid that night, you can't even prove I was there. I haven't done anything wrong."

Win took the camera off of the tripod and tossed it from hand to hand, Arnold made to get up as though wanting to snatch it back and Win stepped back shaking his head.

"I'd recommend staying exactly where you are Arnold, it wouldn't take much for me to lose my grip and accidentally drop this expensive bit of kit."

He could see the panic growing on Arnold's face, so he pushed him a bit harder.

"If you did have some photos of that night, it would be most helpful. It might mean I could turn a blind eye to all of the breaches I can see here. Imagine if I called my colleagues and told them to check what it was you ferreted away under your pillow when I came in. I bet they'd want to search everywhere after finding that, all your digital photos would be found. They'd even turn your mum's room over; you wouldn't have hidden anything in there would you?"

Arnold was breathing heavily by now; he'd tugged the sheet right over himself and was almost hiding behind it.

"No need for any of that officer. I'm sure I can think of a way to help you out. If you look in the second drawer down each photo pack is dated, you might find something helpful."

Win kept hold of the camera as he opened the drawer, packs, and packs of developed photos were neatly lined up in date order.

Plucking one out he could see that Arnold had helpfully added the location to the front, putting that one back he worked along until he found the pack with the right date and location.

Putting that pack in his pocket he offered Arnold a smile.

"Wasn't too difficult, was it?"

"Is that everything?"

Arnold's voice was small, not much above a husky whisper, oh yes, this man had secrets he didn't want to be found, thought Win grimly.

"Yes thanks, Mr. Green, you've been most helpful."

Phelps made for the door, but as his hand touched the handle to let himself out Arnold called over to him.

"What about my camera DCI Phelps? It's worth a lot of money."

"I think I'll keep hold of this for a bit Arnold, just to keep you honest you understand. I wouldn't want you to be tempted to take any photos you shouldn't."

Before the man could protest, Win let himself out and slammed the door closed behind him.

Mrs. Green was still hanging around the hall, wringing her hands and looking as though the weight of the world was on her shoulders.

Win tried to dig up some sympathy for her but found he was empty, she must know what he was up to, he thought.

She just digs her head in the sand and pretends there's nothing wrong while he's photographing her neighbour's kids.

Ignoring her Win let himself out, he took a big gulp of the clean night air to clear the filth from his lungs from being in that house.

Pulling out his mobile he put in a call to Steph, there was no way he was leaving that man unmonitored right next to a park.

Terry waited until his wife fell asleep before silently dressing in a dark tracksuit and trainers.

Finding an old rucksack in the cupboard he filled it with the tools he'd need to break into Win's house and a torch.

Adding a heavy hammer, he smiled unpleasantly to himself, the old man had better hope he sleeps through, he thought grimly.

He'd also purchased a black balaclava earlier; he folded it over the top of his head like a hat.

He moved silently through the kitchen and out of the backdoor, ignoring his car, the engine starting might wake Rachel, and he jogged away up the road.

Walking through the gates into the fair gave Andy a flashback.

There he was, 10 years old, holding his mum's hand while his sister held dad's, and as soon as they'd got in he'd yanked free and started hopping up and down excitedly.

From the look on his friend's faces, they were also taking a time trip back to more innocent days.

They retraced their steps back to the ghost train, the whole place was set up much as it had been thirty years ago,

Andy stood in the small clearing where Terry had knocked him down.

He spun in a slow circle, the last time he'd seen his sister, the place where her small hand had slipped out of his.

Spotting a booth the group ran over, the man behind the plastic sheeting looked in his fifties, and he shook his head at them.

"Sorry guys, you're too old for this ride, kiddies only."

Derek gave him a smile and as if by magic a twenty-pound note appeared in his hand, he slipped it under the gap.

The man narrowed his eyes suspiciously.

"You can't want to go on it that much surely?"

"Actually, we're looking for a bit of information. We're looking for a man called Jay, he'd have been working here thirty years ago when Willow Gardner went missing."

The man reared back as though Derek had physically slapped him, his gaze skittered over the group in front of his booth, until they alighted on Andy.

At this point, he scooped up the note, stood up, and left the booth locking the door behind him.

"Follow me."

They didn't have to go far, behind the ride was a little clearing, foldout camping chairs, and a small camping table that hinted it might be where the fair folk went for a break. The man pulled out a pack of cigs and lit one up, taking a deep drag he focused on Andy again.

"I never forget a face, it's all part of the job. You're that kid's brother, right?"

Andy nodded, and the man rubbed his chin, the bristles rasped on his rough skin.

"I'm Jay, and I've been waiting for this moment for thirty years. I hoped someone might come back."

The group felt a spark, this sounded promising, but Jay quickly shook his head.

"What I mean is that what I saw wasn't anything to do with Willow. I've worried all these years that it might get given more significance than it deserves, and your family deserved better."

Andy looked puzzled, "You saw a kid that might have been Willow, right?"

Jay sighed, "I think the police were wondering if the kid I saw was Willow with her hair shaved and wearing boy's clothes. I thought about that all night, then the same kid came back a few nights later. Mum was still bad-tempered and mean, the kid had home-cut hair but was definitely a boy, and definitely her son. I'm sorry mate, but if you've pinned your hopes on this then it's not the lead you think it was."

Andy felt the sting of disappointment, Jay read it in his face and awkwardly clapped his shoulder with his hand.

"I am sorry, I had a little sister around that age too and I'd have given my left nut to get yours back for you, I knew exactly how you must've felt. My parents were gutted, they talked about nothing else for months. We all felt it as though it was one of our own."

The group felt gutted, one less lead to follow up and it wasn't as though there were many to start with.

Win put his book to one side when his mobile rang.

He'd taken himself off to bed when he'd got home, as tempting as it had been to look through those photos straight away, he knew it was best done with rested eyes.

He could see from the screen it was Steph, he answered with his usual, "Phelps."

"Nice little stash we found boss."

Phelps couldn't help the grin at the familiar address, it wasn't his role anymore, but he liked that she still saw him that way.

"Drawers full of photos dating way back, other drawers with rows and rows of saved digital files, and to top it all for him, several magazines featuring underage photos of an explicit nature. We've got enough to make sure he's kept out of the way for a long time."

There was a pause, he could hear her breathing, and the faint background noise of officers talking to each other. She was calling from the scene.

"Interesting how you came across this information boss. Also interesting is that it looked as though one pack of photos was missing, there was a gap where they should've been. The little shit is squealing like a pig, so I thought I'd give you the heads up that DCI Brooks is likely to want a word."

"Any chance you can put him off for a bit?"

Win didn't want to get into the missing photo pack with her. He liked her too much to lie to her, but he also couldn't tell her the truth yet.

"No chance boss, he's going to want to know how we found out about this haul. Even if I tell him, it was an anonymous call, Squealy Green will spill the beans about your visit, and I'll be left with egg on my face."

Win silently cussed to himself, Brooks would not be best pleased to find out he'd also neglected to add his retired status when he went to the house earlier.

"I may have forgotten to mention that I was retired."

Steph was silent again; he could imagine her expression of annoyance at this additional information.

"Shit boss, Brooks won't be pleased about that at all. Okay, well, what's done is done, and we've got someone nasty off the streets as a result. I'll do my best to smooth it over, but you can definitely expect a visit from him."

Win heard someone call her name in the background.

"Look, I've got to go, they need me to coordinate the collection of the evidence. Speak to you later."

After the call, he tried to pick his book back up, but the words all seemed to run into one. After reading the same paragraph three times without taking it in he closed it around the bookmark.

Placing the book back on his bedside table he realised the case had taken over his life again, and it was all he could think about.

Sighing in frustration Win felt around on the side table for the television handset, maybe some background noise would help him fall asleep.

Fluffing up his pillows and rolling the duvet around him he tried to force himself to focus on the screen, but instead, his mind kept wandering back to Willow.

Kicking off the covers he dug about in his bedside drawer until he came across a pad and pen, he may as well start writing down the thoughts bubbling in his head in the hopes that would help him settle.

Where to start? A timeline, he thought.

Always Win's go-to, for some reason seeing everything in order helped him find the holes, and the questions that needed answering.

7 pm – Andy and Willow are seen on the throw-a-hoop stall where he wins her a cuddly rabbit

7.30 pm – Andy gets into a fight with Terry and his friends, he lets go of Willow's hand and this is the last time he sees her.

7.35 p.m. – Willow is seen by Margo Granger apparently heading in the direction of the public toilets – the statement says she was definitely alone at this point.

7.45 pm – Andy realises she's missing, and the boys start looking for her – they speak to Margo, and she tells them about a little girl in red shorts heading in the direction of the toilets.

7.50.pm – Andy and his friends find the torn red shorts and alert his parents who call the police

7.55 p.m. – Jay, the fairground worker, claims to have seen a kid with shaved hair being dragged out of the fair by an unknown woman.

8.05.pm – Police close down the fair – no one in or out

8.10.pm – Search undertaken of the toilets, sink full of blonde curls and smears of blood found. No sign of Willow or the toy that her brother won for her earlier that evening.

Win could've cried in frustration, it was no more helpful now than it had been all those years ago, nothing was jumping out at him.

He thought for a moment, could he insert some approximate times around the other boy's movements?

Terry and his crowd hadn't hung around after jumping Andy, they'd apparently scuttled off in the same direction that Willow was seen to be heading only a few minutes before them.

So that meant that at some point after 7.40 one or all of those boys could have had the opportunity to see Willow marching off to the toilets on her own.

That was the idea that kept trying to break through, he thought.

Tomorrow morning he'd arrange to see Terry again, and this time he was going to push him into telling the truth.

Chapter 14

The sash window posed no problem for Terry, a little tinkering, and he was soon able to push it up and climb silently into the living room.

He flashed his torch around to get his bearings, the room was neat and well-organised, and Terry knew he'd have to be careful not to disrupt anything too much in his search.

His beam lit up a large desk that appeared to be the focal point of the room, that's the best place to start, he thought.

Feeling around under the desk he didn't find anywhere files and paperwork could be hidden, flashing the light around the room he looked for a file cabinet or a cupboard.

Nothing.

His balaclava was starting to itch his face and Terry was feeling irritated, he'd just wanted to get in and out.

Moving silently to the next room he found a small, office-like area and he headed straight over to the stacks of boxes against the wall.

Just as he'd thought, each one was clearly dated and linked to the case it contained, now it was simply finding the right one.

Retired DCI Phelps helpfully kept them all in date order, which was of big help to Terry.

It didn't take much to find the right boxes and start checking the cases on them.

Terry nearly threw his torch down in frustration, there was a gap where Willow's case box should be.

Shit, shit, shit, he thought angrily, if it's not here, then where is it?

Desperately needing that box, he started his check again, this time from the start, maybe the old man had moved it recently?

Checking his thick gloves were securely on his hands to avoid leaving fingerprints, he started to unstack the boxes for a closer look.

He was so engrossed in his task he didn't hear the occupant of the house approach.

Win had woken with a dry mouth, deciding he couldn't get back to sleep until he got a glass of water, he'd headed downstairs.

When he'd seen the torch light bouncing around the living room, he'd picked up a heavy lamp base and melted back into the shadows.

The figure came out of the living room muting the torch with his hands until he got to the next room.

He, thought Win, the figure was definitely a man's height and build.

Biding his time until he had a good opportunity to catch the intruder unawares, he remained in the shadows, holding his breath so he wouldn't be heard.

Phelps could hear the rustling of boxes being moved, why would a burglar ignore everything of value in the house and go straight to his old case files?

It had to be someone wanting to know what he knew about one of them, and the only one that was currently of interest was Willow's case.

If that's what he's after, thought Win, he's shit out of luck, thank God, I left it at Derek's place earlier.

The photos he'd filched off Green were safely in his bedside table drawer, and Win had no intention of letting the man get upstairs.

Creeping forward towards the room he used as a storage/office, he could see the torch beam was being focused on each box as the intruder checked the dates and cases.

He hefted the lamp base, getting a good grip, he planned to crack the man across the head and then call it in to 999.

Unfortunately, his plan was derailed at the last moment.

A floorboard squeaked under foot; a noise that was barely noticeable during the day suddenly sounded as loud as a bomb going off.

The intruder spun around, and Win swung the lamp base at him. He was off target and instead of hitting him in the head it caught him somewhere softer, from the oomph he heard it must have hurt, he thought with satisfaction.

The intruder still had the heavy torch in his hand, he swiped out with it, and Win tried to dodge to one side, but it still caught him on his shoulder causing a flash of pain that knocked his focus.

Taking advantage of Win's disorientation, the figure shoved him hard, already off-balance Win felt himself falling backward.

He heard the muffled sound of running footsteps before his head cracked against the skirting board.

DCI Brooks and Steph pulled up outside Win's house.

Steph wasn't entirely comfortable with the idea of taking the retired detective by surprise with a visit this late at night, but Brooks had insisted.

"Hopefully, we can get more out of him if he's just been woken up."

Steph had nodded in agreement but knew that her DCI was underestimating Phelps, nothing dampened that sharp mind, not even being dropped in on at this time of night.

Brooks had jumped out of the car first and she was just climbing out of the passenger side when a figure in black appeared to climb out of Win's window and run across the garden.

Whoever it was, was so preoccupied with escape they didn't notice the two officers watching.

Brooks shook off his surprise, and immediately headed towards the figure who was by now aware of their presence as he legged it up the road as fast as his legs could carry him.

Someone athletic, mused Steph as she watched him easily outrun her DCI.

Walking up to the front door she pressed the doorbell and knocked a few times but there was no response.

By now Brooks had joined her, panting and out of breath he eyed the door, reluctant to try and put it in but not seeing any other way of gaining access.

Steph shook her head, "Hold on boss."

She made her way across the garden and lifted a gnome, before fishing out the spare key he was sitting on.

Waving it at Brooks, she used it to let them into the house.

The living room wasn't occupied, nothing looked touched either which made Steph frown.

What sort of burglar didn't turn over the main room in the house?

The next room was fairly small and looked as though it was used for storage mostly, Steph raced forwards when she saw Win slumped on the floor.

Blood pooled under his head and smeared the white skirting boards.

The man himself was pale and unresponsive, she bent down and was relieved when his breath tickled her cheek.

Phelps let out a groan and struggled to sit up, Steph and Brooks took an arm each and helped him to his feet.

Win wobbled slightly as they walked him over to a chair and supported him while he sat in it.

Steph nipped to the kitchen and dampened a tea towel under the tap, handing it to him he clutched it to the side of his head that had hit the skirting boards.

Pulling it away and seeing the red stain spreading across it he winced.

"Bastard clumped me with his torch then shoved me over."

His words were slightly slurred, and Steph suggested that they call an ambulance, but Win snorted.

"Don't you bloody dare. I'll be fine if you could get me a nice, sweet cup of tea, that'll set me straight."

Brooks didn't comment on the retired detective's stubbornness, if he was honest, he admired it.

"We came round to ask you how you came to know so much about Albert Green, we'd just pulled up and we saw the little fucker climbing out of your window and legging it up the street. I did go after him, but he had too much of a head start."

Steph hid a smile; Brooks obviously didn't want to admit he'd been outrun.

She got the impression that Win had read the situation too, but to his credit, he didn't dispute it either.

Brooks turned his gaze around the room before alighting on Win.

"Strange nothing was taken, and the house wasn't turned over. Unusual burglar."

Phelps shrugged as though unconcerned.

"Maybe I disturbed him before he could steal anything? Then when he thought he'd hurt me he legged it."

Brooks gave Phelps a longer look, his small smile showed that he didn't believe that scenario at all.

"Maybe that's it. Or maybe it's because you're sticking your nose in where it doesn't belong?"

Win set his face in a look of innocence that almost made Steph laugh again.

"I have no idea what you're talking about Brooks"

Her DCI let it slide without a direct challenge but did move back to talking about Arnold Green.

"Any comment on why Arnold Green is shouting your name from one end of the station to the other? He seems to be under the impression that you're still a serving officer, and I'm very interested in the "anonymous tip" that led us right to him."

Win shrugged, "Maybe he wasn't listening to me when I told him I was retired when we met, and I'm not sure why I'd know anything about your anonymous tip."

Brooks shook his head in disbelief, it looked as though Win wasn't intending to be helpful.

"I'm going to be blunt. Are you looking into Willow Gardner's case?"

Phelps looked thoughtful as he weighed up how to answer such a direct question without blatantly lying.

"I've spoken to her brother a couple of times since he came back to town, you know what it's like with that one case that got away."

Win was clearly hoping that a generalised answer would be enough to put Brooks off.

"Phelps, I'm not sold. I think you're up to something and I think you're stepping on my toes. I appreciate the heads up about Green, anything that gets him off the streets is most welcome, but I'm not so appreciative of you stomping around pretending you're not retired."

Brooks left that hanging in the air, clearly hopeful that the words would reach their target. Win fixed his face into his innocent, no idea what you're talking about, expression.

Stalemate, thought Steph with interest, wonder how this'll end.

It ended with both men giving each other a look that suggested they knew what the other was up to.

After they'd gone, Win leaned back in his chair.

His head was pounding, and he was going to need to take some paracetamol before bed, but he kept running the figure through his head.

With his build and the athletic way he outran Brooks, they all suggested Terry as the prime suspect.

The question was, why would Terry need to break into his house, and what was he looking for?

Chapter 15

Terry was fit for his age, the weekends playing football and jogging every morning kept him in shape.

Even so, he was out of puff when he got back to his house, breathing heavily he let himself in, and carefully eased the door closed so his nosy wife didn't hear it.

He'd bagged up his clothes and balaclava and planned to dispose of them the next day.

Wearing just his pants and an old T-shirt he'd leaned against the sink downing a glass of water, his heart still racing from the close call earlier.

He'd overslept the next morning, and using his mother's accident as an excuse, he called work and arranged for the deputy head to take over the school for the day.

Rachel had already left for work when he got downstairs so he made himself a mug of coffee and pushed a couple of slices of bread into the toaster just as the doorbell sounded.

Tying his dressing gown cord a bit tighter, and assuming it must be the postman, he flung the door open.

Seeing Win on the doorstep gave him a moment of panic, he quickly settled his expression to one of puzzlement and hoped the retired officer hadn't picked up on it.

"To what do I owe the dubious pleasure of an early morning visit from our local retired police detective?"

Win smiled at him, and Terry took note that it was a policeman's professional smile.

The one that didn't touch the eyes, the one that suggested that the owner knew something about the recipient.

"Can we speak indoors Mr Peck?"

Knowing that to refuse would be to look guilty of something Terry reluctantly let Phelps into the house. In the kitchen, he sipped his now lukewarm coffee without offering to make a cup for his guest.

The toaster popped and Win directed his gaze towards it.

"Have I interrupted your breakfast, Mr. Peck?"

Win's tone suggested he wasn't concerned if he had, and Terry shrugged in response.

"No work today, Mr. Peck? I wasn't aware it was a school holiday?"

"My mother had an unfortunate accident yesterday and I was at the hospital until late, my deputy is covering for me today so I can go and check on her."

Terry looked pointedly at the clock on the wall, clearly hinting that he had plans and Win was interrupting them.

"I'm sorry to hear that Mr. Peck, I'll try not to take up too much of your time."

To avoid Phelps' intense look, Terry drifted over to the toaster and removed the now cold toast.

As though it had a mind of its own, his hand touched the side of the toaster.

The lightning bolt of electricity shot up his arm and made his eyes roll back.

Terry had a feeling as though he was flying through the air.

His head jerked backward as he landed on the opposite side of the room, hitting the solid wall by the door with a dull crack.

The next he knew Win was crouched down next to him reaching out as though to check he was still breathing.

Terry shook his head to clear the fog, it wouldn't do to speak without thinking clearly.

"I'm fine. The toaster must be faulty."

Phelps looked more interested than sympathetic.

"Shall I call an ambulance sir?"

"No thanks, I'm fine, just a small shock from a domestic appliance."

To prove his point Terry struggled clumsily to his feet and hobbled over to one of the chairs around the kitchen table.

He could hear Win running the tap and opening the cupboards before placing a glass of water in front of him.

"Strangest thing happened to me last night. Someone broke into my house, they didn't take anything, but they seemed to be looking for something specific."

Win's gaze dropped to the large patch of bruising coming up on Terry's shoulder, clearly visible as his dressing gown had slipped during his fall.

"I clumped the bloke with a lamp base, he managed to avoid being hit in the head, but I caught him hard on his shoulder. I'd imagine he's got quite the bruise to show for it."

Terry yanked his dressing gown back up and managed a nonchalant shrug.

"If you're referring to my bruise then I'd imagine that was from my accident just now."

"It wouldn't have come out that quickly Mr. Peck."

Terry occupied himself gulping down some more water while he came up with something else.

"Then it's from a rough tackle at five-a-side over the weekend. Why would I be prowling around your house Mr. Phelps? I'm a respectable head teacher, not a burglar."

Win gave a half smile, one that suggested he wasn't buying what Terry was trying to sell him.

"A lot of strange things happening lately don't you think?"

Terry hoped he was keeping his face straight, but his thoughts were racing.

"Not really."

Phelps changed tact, hoping that he could throw Terry off enough to get a more honest answer out of him.

"Were you surprised to hear about Frank's death?"

He saw the man's adam's apple rise and fall as he swallowed, and the ultimate sign of someone nervous, his tongue flicking out and wetting his dry lips, but when Terry spoke, he still managed to sound unconcerned.

"Fat man dies of a heart attack. Not exactly headline news, is it?"

"And George?"

"George was an unhappy man, demonstrated by the fact that he ended up killing himself. Nothing strange, just very sad."

"Margo Gardner?"

Terry's lip curled slightly, but that was the only sign he was getting irritated.

"Woman in heels falls down her stairs, again not exactly a shocker headline is it."

Phelps sat in silence for a moment, letting it build in the hope that Terry would fill it.

Terry just got up and refilled his glass of water.

"Thank you for your assistance earlier Mr. Phelps, if there's nothing else, I need to get showered and dressed so I can go and visit my mother."

Win stood, but before he left, he offered one final parting shot.

"Lucky I was here Mr. Peck, maybe next time you won't be so lucky, and I'm pretty sure there will be a next time. Until you tell me the truth, you'll need to keep looking over your shoulder, waiting for the next "accident." Do yourself a favour, in fact, do your family a favour, and tell me what happened to Willow. I'll leave you to think about that, send my best to your mother."

Terry heard the front door close behind the retired detective, and he poured the unwanted water down the sink.

He could feel the world closing in on him, there were too many "accidents" for him to feel safe.

Phelps was right about one thing, he was constantly looking over his shoulder, but there was no way he was going to be pushed into talking either.

He'd kept the secret for thirty years.

Thirty years of building himself a life, and no one was going to take that away from him.

At first glance, you'd think he hadn't got much out of Terry earlier, but as someone who could read a suspect's micro-expressions like an open book, Win was even more certain he knew something.

Brooks would blow a gasket if he knew Win was still poking around, Phelps smiled, he liked the bloke, but this case was eating him alive.

He'd do whatever it took to solve it, and if that involved standing back and waiting for another "misfortune" to hit Terry so be it.

Letting himself back into his house he plodded upstairs and retrieved the pack of photos from his bedside table drawer before picking up his mobile.

Many eyes would make lighter work of seeing if there was anything of value in them.

Pressing the saved contact for Andy he asked if the group would like to come to his or if he should come to them.

Chapter 16

They were all sat in Derek's living room, each had a handful of photos in front of them and there was silence as they peered closely looking for anyone familiar.

Steve frowned at his collection.

"Where did you get these from? Someone seems to have taken a lot of photos of random kids?"

Phelps decided to be semi-honest in his answer.

"As I told you before, we looked closely at the known paedophiles in the area and these photos turned up recently. I thought they might help."

Steve shot him a suspicious look, as someone who'd had the most dealings with the police in the group, he was more aware of how they worked, and there was something about what Phelps was telling them that didn't ring true to him.

As far as he could see all the kids in the photos were around the same age, 3 years up to 6 years old, and a mixture of boys and girls.

The person taking the photos hadn't focused on their faces as most people would've, they'd taken candid body shots, usually when a child was climbing or on a ride.

It made him feel sick looking at them, someone had taken these for their own sick pleasure.

Forcing himself to keep going for Andy's sake, he couldn't help but hope that it wasn't someone like that who'd taken poor Willow.

Ten photos in, and Steve hadn't seen her, there were only five more to go in his set when a figure in the background caught his eye.

"Has anyone got a magnifying glass?"

The group looked around when Steve called out, and Derek rummaged in a drawer until he found what Steve had asked for.

They huddled around him as he peered closely at the image, and when he confirmed what he'd seen his hand shook so hard he could barely hold onto to magnifying glass.

Unable to find the words, he silently handed it to Andy and pushed the photo toward him.

Andy bent over, and there, in her familiar bright red shorts, with her blonde curls bouncing was Willow.

Her tiny hand was held by another familiar figure, the rotund Frank was clearly distinguishable.

Andy dropped the magnifying glass, his face went white, and he looked as though he might be about to throw up.

Derek quickly put a chair behind him and gently pushed him into it.

Win snatched up the glass and took a look for himself, he sighed as he got a magnified view of the pair.

The older boy was looking down at the little girl, his face caught in profile in the shot, his mouth open slightly as though he was speaking to her.

None of the other boys were in view, but looking closer Win was sure he could see a pair of trainer-clad toes, but the rest of the boy was out of shot.

Holding the glass over that part of the photo he asked Derek what he thought, wondering if he'd recognise them.

"I can't say for sure, but see here?"

Derek pointed to something that appeared to be attached to the laces.

"That looks like the bottle tops that Terry used to put on his laces, a few kids did it so it's not definitive it was him, but considering that where you saw one, you'd see the others, I'd guess it's pretty likely."

There was silence while they all considered this, there was no disputing that Frank was involved, there he was, holding Willow's hand and chatting with her.

The issue was, did the other two boys know, and if they did, what were they covering up?

Arthur Peck was looking at his favourite fishing website while sitting on the toilet.

It was often the only place he got any peace and quiet from his constantly complaining wife.

Scrolling through the pictures of fishing equipment on the site he mentally listed all the things he wanted to get before the next season on his lake started.

Angling was the only other way he got a break from the domineering woman he'd married.

Sitting on the bank, rods in the water, and cold ciders in a cool box next to him, he could daydream about a life that didn't involve being a henpecked coward.

Elizabeth hadn't been that way when he'd met her, she wasn't the prettiest woman on offer, but she was handsome and witty.

He'd rushed into marrying her when she'd announced she was expecting, it was the way things were back then. you didn't leave a woman unwed if she got in the family way.

Everything was fine until the little prince was born.

Terry had arrived, kicking and screaming, into the world, his wrinkled little face puce and his cries merely the mews of a newborn.

As time had gone on, Terry had become increasingly demanding, and Elizabeth had rushed to respond to his every need as though to make him wait would be to fall short of her role as his mother.

In return, Terry had the expectation of his mother appearing every time he so much as opened his mouth.

Arthur loved his son, of course, he did, but the boy was spoiled and overindulged by his doting mother. It made the boy unkind and cruel to others.

A school counselor had once hesitantly addressed the problem with them at a parent/teacher conference.

The young woman had cloaked her true feelings in all the right words.

"Terry is bright, and he has an excellent vocabulary, but his lack of social links seems to make him isolated and unhappy."

Arthur had immediately understood what she was trying to say, his son had no friends and was a smartarse with the teachers.

He'd heard it from every single one he'd spoken to that night, and by this time was prickling with embarrassment and shame that a child of his was so much of a burden on the school system.

Elizabeth, on the other hand, wasn't at all concerned, if anything she was irritated by what she called, "the small-mindedness of the staff."

She'd held her tongue reluctantly as they'd moved from desk to desk, but this well-meaning young lady was the straw that broke the camel's back.

Elizabeth had been defensive and rude, her tone was sharp and unforgiving, and the young woman had cringed away from them.

Her pale face was blotchy with patches of red as she tried to explain what she meant.

Arthur was tempted to offer her a shovel to dig her hole a bit deeper, but he decided that discretion was the better part of valour.

He had to live with the woman and upsetting Liz would mean weeks of sulking and digs.

So, he'd stayed quiet and allowed his wife to tear the poor young teacher to shreds, and he hadn't said a word until they left.

He waited until they were all back in the car, Terry strapped in the back and his wife sat beside him, her back ramrod straight and her face a picture of indignation at what she saw as an unfair description of her little prince.

Arthur had intended to keep his peace, keep quiet like he always did, and suck it up.

It was looking at Terry's smug smile in the rear-view mirror that changed his mind.

"When we get home, I'm going to want an explanation from you boy, and if you think you can fob me off like you do your mother, you're very much mistaken. Unless you can come up with one good reason why you behave so badly at school, I will be taking my belt to you, and you can forget seeing any of the other kids for the foreseeable."

The last part was a routine Arthur followed, he was aware that it wasn't much of a threat, Terry's only friends were the other two unpleasant bullies that he hung around with, but it felt parental to say it to him.

The journey home was filled with cold silence, his wife shooting him daggers, and Terry pretending to snivel in the backseat to keep her riled up.

As soon as they got in the house the games began.

Terry played one of his trump cards first, standing outside the front door he quivered and shook, crocodile tears streaming down his cheeks.

"Don't make me go in mum, please. He's going to beat me with a belt, please don't make me go indoors, I'm so scared."

Arthur had ignored the look his wife shot him, he was already growing immune to it, and this time he was determined to do his duty as a father.

Grabbing his whining son by his upper arm he dragged him through the front door and dumped him unceremoniously in the armchair in the living room.

By this time Terry was bawling, his little skinny legs and feet were drumming against the chair as he waved his arms in the air.

It was too much for his doting mother.

She ran between them, facing Arthur with a look of determination on her face.

"You will not touch our son Arthur."

He'd thrown her a scornful look and shoved her easily to one side; he'd slowly unbuckled his belt and pulled it through the tags on his trousers.

Terry had continued to make the same noise, but Arthur noticed there were no tears and a look of amused interest in his eyes.

That was the moment that he'd realised that his son was a monster, a psychopath who lacked the normal emotional capacity and warmth of others.

Deep down he knew the beating wouldn't do any good, it was too late, born or created, it made no odds.

Terry was beyond help and a few whacks with a belt wouldn't change that.

Not a man to back down, not then anyway, he'd gone through with it.

Grasping his son firmly by the arms he'd thrown him over his knee and yanked his school trousers down.

Winding the belt around his fist he'd given him a few lashes, pulling back at the last minute so as not to hurt him too much, but hoping the sting might just make a point.

At first, Elizabeth grabbed his arm and tried to beg him to stop, but when he stoically ignored her and pushed her away, she fled out of the room in tears.

Without his mother, for an audience, Terry's wails and protests had completely stopped, he lay across Arthur's lap and took every lash without a sound.

Unable to keep up the anger he needed to continue he'd pushed the boy from his knees and allowed him to fall to the floor.

Terry had jumped up, pulled up his trousers, and then shrugged, before leaving the room after his mother.

No one in the household ever mentioned it again. Liz had blanked him for a few weeks, and he'd seen from the smirk on Terry's face he was enjoying the way he'd got between them.

Arthur told himself he didn't care, he didn't feel bad about it, and he was just doing his fatherly duty.

Despite that, Arthur had never attempted to punish Terry again, he'd fallen back into the peripherals of family life, and there he'd stayed.

He'd had years of watching Terry's behaviour get more and more concerning, like the local pets they found dead, and the bullying at school.

Arthur had silently watched, he'd known that the day would come when Terry went too far, but even he hadn't been prepared for just how far he could go.

Knowing his wife wouldn't tolerate his absence for much longer, he prepared to close down the site on his phone and stroll back out of the bathroom.

Standing up and flushing the chain, despite not even using it, he went to run the tap.

His wife would be all over him if she thought he'd left the bathroom without washing his hands and she had ears like a bat.

Arthur twisted the top of the hot tap and let the water flow into the sink, as it heated up the mirror steamed over. Staring at it for something to do while he waited, he jumped as he saw words appear in the misty overlay.

YOU WILL ALL PAY

He stared at the words in horror, they were somehow childlike, as though written by a small, child's hand. That thought sent a wave of panic through him, his stomach clenched, and he felt physically sick.

Frozen to the spot by fear the water continued to gush into the drain.

"I'm sorry."

Arthur stuttered this out of his dry lips, hoping that whatever it was that had come for him would accept his apology.

His hand reached out as though it had a mind of its own, grasping the old-fashioned, wet-shave razor that his son had bought him one Christmas.

Not a man to bother with all that he'd thanked him profusely but then left the kit unused on the marble top that surrounded the sink.

He felt his fingers close around the cold, metal handle, before bringing the sharp blade up toward his face.

He wanted to put it down, to pull his head back before it could reach him, but he couldn't move an inch.

Arthur felt the sharp blade touch him above his adam's apple, it was cold, and as he exerted a little pressure the small cut stung.

In the mirror, he watched as blood blossomed behind the razor, and he winced again.

Arthur was sure he felt a very small, cold hand, over his, the hand pushed down harder, but he was unable to put up any resistance.

The blade sliced into the wrinkled folds of skin that hung over his throat and easily pared through it.

Blood was now pouring from the wound he'd made; it ran down his neck and flooded his camouflage T-shirt until the top half was soaked red.

Surprisingly, he didn't feel any pain, just a strange feeling as though he was removed from what was going on.

The cut looked like a large extra mouth across his neck, in fact with the curve on either side it looked very much like a smile, he thought.

The pain when it started, wasn't from the wound, it was a flash from right under his ribcage that radiated up his left arm.

His heart, he thought, all those years of not caring for myself have come up on top.

The words on the mirror swam in front of his eyes, for some reason his vision was blurred, and he couldn't seem to read them anymore.

When his legs gave way, Arthur had the impression of falling through sticky treacle, it was almost comforting.

That was until his head slammed into the toilet base.

Chapter 17

Brooks looked around the blood-spattered bathroom and couldn't help the disgust that crawled through his guts.

It was everywhere, across the mirror where the man had stood when he slit his own throat and all across the floor after he'd collapsed from the blood loss.

Mrs Peck's pastel pink and light blue matching bathroom rugs were unrecognisable and beyond saving.

The woman herself had told him that when her husband didn't return from his visit to the bathroom, she'd gone to find out what was keeping him.

Hearing the running water but not getting a reply when she called his name, she'd burst into the unlocked room to discover a scene that resembled an abattoir.

Her husband was lying in a crumpled heap around the base of the toilet, the pool of blood around him obscuring the wound that had finished him off.

Fearing he'd had a bad fall she'd immediately called for an ambulance.

The paramedics pronounced him dead; they'd spotted the neck wound and immediately reported it as an unexpected death triggering the police response.

Brooks had heard it go out over the police radio and recognising the name had decided to go along and see what was what.

Now here he was, standing at the site of what at first glance looked like a suicide.

Brooks took a quick glance around; the old-fashioned razor had clattered into the sink when Mr. Peck had lost the ability to grip it any longer.

Its long, curved blade was stained with his blood, despite the hot water running into the sink for so long.

He almost missed it, if he hadn't looked up at the red-stained mirror he'd have left without noting it and a vital clue would've been left off.

The tap had been shut off by the paramedics, but despite the mirror clearing of steam the words that had been written in it remained visible on the glass.

YOU WILL ALL PAY

Now that put a different light on things, thought Brooks, looked more as though there was a motive to do Mr. Peck harm than a bog-standard suicide.

Pay for what though?

As far as he knew, Mr. Peck's run through the system had bought up nothing of interest, no complaints, no investigations, and certainly no offenses.

"I wonder if it's got anything to do with the Gardner cold case, sir?"

Steph had appeared behind him; she was looking at the words with interest and waiting for his reply.

"What makes you think that?"

Steph shrugged, "The other two men who died were friends of Terry Peck's, now his dad has died too, and I heard his mum had a bad accident at the weekend as well. Lots of coincidences sir. Add in that Gardner woman and it looks like everyone involved in the original case is getting bumped off."

Brooks took that onboard, he wasn't a superstitious man by nature, but he was also open-minded enough to look into any clue or possible scenario that came up, even an unlikely link to a thirty-year-old missing child case.

"Maybe we should be speaking to retired DCI Phelps and those other people he's been hanging around with. Check out why her brother is back in town and linked up with his old friends. Also, I'd like to know more about the woman in the group, she wasn't born around here, what's her link?"

Both officers stared at the fading words for a while longer, and Steph pulled out her mobile to snap a couple of shots before they were lost forever.

No other photos of interest had shown up in the batches that Win had handed out to the group, he put them all away apart from the one with Frank holding Willow's hand.

Evan spoke up first, breaking the heavy silence that had fallen over the room.

"I've got a contact who can blow that up and focus on the part we're interested in; do you want me to call her?"

With no dissenters in the room, Evan pulled out his mobile and flicked through his contacts until he found the one, he wanted.

"Hey there Helen, it's Evan. Yes, I know, and I fully intend to keep my word."

He gave a flirty chuckle that made Derek shake his head in mock disapproval.

"I've actually got another favour to ask, it'll mean a far more expensive dinner rather than just a lunch, what do you say? It's nothing massive, just a photo I need blowing up so we can get a bit of detail on a background image."

Everyone looked at him expectantly while they waited for the outcome, after more back-and-forth innuendo, his warm thank you seemed to suggest he'd got what he wanted.

"It's a go, I just have to meet up with Helen and pass over the original, she'll make a copy and then blow one up for us."

Win looked less pleased than Evan thought he would, in fact, he was frowning at the photo in his hand.

"I'm in the shit already, if it gets out that I took evidence, and let civilians look through it I'll be lucky not to face charges of obstructing the case. Add on letting someone take one of the photos and completely breaking the chain of custody, and well, I may as well put the handcuffs on myself."

They all waited while he debated with himself what to do next, Phelps gave a heavy sigh and held the photo out.

"In for a penny, in for a pound, I guess. If we can get a clearer look at that part of the image, we might be able to find something that identifies the foot in the corner."

Evan took it before Win could change his mind, he'd just tucked it into his bag when the doorbell sounded.

The familiar base of Reynold's voice reached them as he let someone in, footsteps across the hall and then the door to the living room opened.

Brooks and Steph were standing behind him, Reynolds gave them a dry, short introduction before turning on his heel and marching off to wherever he spent his time when he wasn't fetching food and drink or answering the door.

Brooks glanced around at each face before his gaze lingered on Phelps for a little longer than the others.

"I thought we'd find you all together. I think it's time we pooled our knowledge, Terry Peck's father was found dead earlier, and I reckon that'll mean something to you all."

The atmosphere crackled with electricity as everyone's attention focused on Brooks.

He took a seat towards the center of the room, crossing his ankle over his knee he leaned back and got comfortable.

"Where shall we start people?"

Brooks pointed at Cleo.

"For starters, who are you, and what do you have to do with all of this?"

Cleo glanced at the group, unsure if she should share her backstory outside of the group, what she'd have to say was hardly easy to believe.

Andy nodded to her, so she took a deep breath to calm her nerves and tried to make her role sound less creepy than it probably was.

"Ever since I was a little girl, I've had messages from those who are no longer with us. Usually, it's simple things, like "tell my husband I loved him", or "let my wife know my will is in the second drawer down in my office." This time it was different. There were enough details to help me to track down Andy and convince him, but since then it's mainly just been different names. I didn't know what those names meant until we all got together, but since then each one has died."

Brooks had been watching her intently the whole time she was speaking, taking in the way she blushed as she spoke and how uncomfortable she was with sharing the details. In his experience, she showed no tells of deception, just a woman uncomfortable with what she had to say.

He sighed, this bloody case was doing his head in.

"Did you get Arthur Peck's name?"

Cleo shook her head

"Nope, in fact, I've had nothing at all since Frank, not even anyone else coming through. It feels as though I'm empty."

Tears stung her eyes; despite the hardships that her gift bought her she was so used to her voices and messages, that losing them was like having a piece of her missing.

"Any idea what the link is to Willow Gardener's case?"

Brooks noticed that Win kept his own face expressionless, but the others looked uncomfortable as though they knew something they didn't want to share.

He narrowed his eyes, and again directed the strength of his stare at Phelps, who to his credit looked away.

"We think the three boys saw something or were somehow involved in Willow going missing."

Win kept it simple, he didn't mention the photo yet, hoping that he could keep that on the down-low until Evan's friend had produced the blown-up version.

"I'd be interested to know who broke into your house, Win."

Brooks had scored.

All the faces in the room turned to look at Phelps showing they hadn't been aware of the break-in.

Since it was the back of his head that took the brunt of the attack by the "burglar" there were no obvious signs for anyone to see and question.

Phelps shrugged, "No idea, I've checked, and it doesn't look as though he or she took anything."

Brooks felt his irritation building, this stupid game needed to end before any more bodies landed on his doorstep.

"For fucks sake man, stop pissing about and cough up."

Win hesitated, but seeing no other way out decided he had no choice but to share it all.

Brooks occasionally interrupted with the odd question, or to clarify a point, but mainly he sat in silence letting the retired detective tell it in his way.

When Phelps had finished there was silence for a moment, even Steph was staring at him incredulously.

"So, you think it was Terry that broke in and cracked you one? This comes from a bruise you saw on his shoulder when you went around his house in clear defiance of my instructions to leave this to the official police?"

Win shrugged and answered a question with a question.

"Would you have believed any of this if I'd told you before?"

Brooks shook his head

"Fair point, probably not, but here we are, with me a reluctant believer. I'm guessing the next task is to talk to Terry?"

"I think his mum might be a better bet, by now she must have the idea that her son is in danger. From meeting her before, I know that Terry is the apple of her eye, it'll be the only way in we've got."

Brooks nodded, "Okay, me and Steph will go with you, just the three of us mind you, we can't show up mob-handed. I'm putting my neck on the line just taking Phelps along. I can also get that photo blown up quicker and more officially than Evan's girlfriend can, so hand it over please."

Brooks scrutinised it closely, he picked up a stray magnifying glass and peered at the little girl in the background before nodding.

"Certainly looks like Willow and Frank."

Brooks stood up and held out his hand to Win.

"Thanks, Phelps, If I'm honest I've always admired you, and I'm actually looking forward to working with you."

He darted Steph a mock, stern, glance.

"I'll even forgive Steph here for her part in sharing information

she shouldn't have."

DS Wright had the grace to blush slightly, but she didn't look too sorry for any of it.

The group was left to their own devices when Win and the other two detectives left the house.

They all felt the same low, it was as though they were suddenly being cut out of the investigation and they didn't know what they should be doing.

Chapter 18

Terry paced from room to room.

His mum was in bits, and whilst Terry wasn't able to feel much about the loss of his father, he didn't like to see his mum upset.

Rachel was sensibly staying out of his way; the anger was etched across his face, and she'd been with him long enough to be wary of him when he was like this.

She didn't understand what was going on but knew there was something more than just the loss of a father he'd barely bothered about when he was alive.

Terry himself was whirring with thoughts, he might have told that retired copper he had no idea what he was talking about, but this was the final nail in the coffin.

Someone must know what really happened that night, someone who was coming after them all one by one.

The only people left alive that knew were him and his mum.

Fucking Frank, he cursed in his head, stupid, fat idiot. This was all his fault, if he wasn't already dead Terry would've gladly finished him off.

Trying to push back his anger so he could think clearly, he took a deep breath and forced himself to unfurl his hands and relax.

Maybe this was for the best?

Without the weaker links, who was left to tell tales?

He'd certainly paid enough over the years, having to get useless George a job at the school and send that waste of space,

Frank, money to keep him when he got too obese to work anymore.

Now both of those burdens were gone, along with the father who'd reluctantly kept schtum.

If he could just stay alive long enough to find out who was behind all of this, it might finally be over.

He'd had thirty years of looking over his shoulder and waiting for it to catch him up with him, it would feel good to be able to move on.

Close the book, turn the page, and start afresh, whatever euphemism you wanted to pick.

A smile lifted his lips, he was the fortunate one, he always had been, and now he was determined to come out on top.

Mrs Peck's hands were steady as she put out cups for her visitors.

Despite the cast on her arm, she'd insisted that she'd supply coffee and biscuits, and as she seemed to need the distraction of doing it all three had agreed.

Win was keeping quiet and letting Brooks take the lead, he didn't have an official standing to be here, and the less obvious he made himself the better.

He didn't reckon on Mrs. Peck recognising him though.

She gave him a long look, one that said she was rooting through her memory for where she knew him from.

"You're that officer that investigated the missing kid case, aren't you? I remember you interviewing my Terry, he was very upset by it all you know."

Phelps nodded; he didn't recall Terry being at all distressed but didn't feel it was a good time to challenge her perception.

"I don't know what any of you want with me now, my husband just killed himself and I'm in no fit state to be answering questions."

Her voice was sharp and despite her words, the loss didn't seem to have affected her as much as they'd expected.

If anything, she was more irritated by their presence than she was by the death of her husband.

"I'm going to have to rely on Terry for everything now. No husband to do the odd jobs around the house anymore, and I can't be expected to pay someone to come in to do them."

Steph tried to make allowances, maybe it was the shock, she thought, but the way it sounded Mrs. Peck was more concerned about the loss of a handyman than a much-loved husband.

Brooks eyed her coolly, he was also surprised by her reaction and decided to throw the words on the mirror out there to see how she responded to them.

It was highly likely she hadn't even seen them herself and might be taken by surprise.

"We attended the scene yesterday, Mrs Peck, there were some strange words on the mirror, it looked as though they'd been written in the steam from the hot water."

"You mean like a suicide note?"

He was right, he mused, she hadn't seen them.

"I wouldn't have said so, they were a bit odd for a suicide note. "You will all pay." Does that mean anything to you?"

Mrs Peck blanched, all the colour leaked from her face leaving her pale, she ran her tongue over her dry lips and her eyes flittered from side to side as though considering what to say next.

"No idea. What a strange thing to write, the poor man can't have been in his right mind."

There was a pitch of anxiety in her tone, the words clearly did mean something to her.

"Yes, Mrs Peck, very strange. So, you've no idea what they were in reference to?"

The older woman's hand shook slightly as she poured coffee into Win's cup, the dark liquid splashed over the rim and onto the pristine white tablecloth.

This gave her an opportunity to avoid answering, she bustled away to the cupboard under the sink and returned with a stain removal spray.

"I must get that straight into soak otherwise I'll never get it out. It's my best tablecloth you know."

Elizabeth knew she was babbling, but her thoughts were all over the place, and she didn't intend to share them with the officers in front of her.

Picking up the cups and moving them out of reach she whipped the cloth off of the table after giving the offending area a good spray.

Turning her back on them she filled the sink with water so she could put it in to soak.

If she was hoping her guests would take the hint and leave, she was going to be disappointed, thought Brooks.

Steph read the situation as well, fetching the cups back she used some coasters to protect the highly polished wood as she handed them back out.

There was a flash of annoyance on the woman's face as she turned back to find them all still settled around her table. She quickly hid it behind a bland mask that reminded Win of her son.

"I'm not sure what you want me to say. It sounds like the ramblings of a disturbed mind, are you trying to suggest it has something to do with that child that went missing? It's been thirty years, surely that's all done and dusted?"

Win couldn't help but take this one, her casual dismissal of a missing five-year-old irked him.

"Willow was never found Mrs. Peck, so the case remains open. The police don't just forget missing children."

With a sly look that suggested she'd hit upon an answer, she widened her eyes as though shocked.

"You're not saying my Arthur had anything to do with that child, are you?

Win could see where she was going with this, if she was hiding something for her son, she'd decided that his father should be put forward for the blame.

"I don't know Mrs. Peck. We didn't have your husband on the suspect list at the time, were either you or he in the vicinity of the fair that night?"

Elizabeth shrugged, "I certainly wasn't, I was home watching tele all night. Arthur did go out at one point, he said he was picking up some milk from the all-night garage, but he did take quite a long time to come back. I'd fallen asleep waiting for him."

"Are you saying that your husband may have been involved with the case Mrs. Peck? You didn't say anything at the time."

Mrs. Peck waved her hand dismissively at them.

"Well, it never occurred to me then, it's now that you're telling me about those words on the mirror that I've started wondering."

Win decided to play the woman at her own game, feigning his own nonchalant shrug, he pushed his coffee cup aside as though getting ready to leave.

"It's something we'll be looking into then. In the meantime, at least we won't have to worry about Terry, the way it looked he was the only one left alive that might know something. We'd thought we needed to make sure he wasn't next on the list, but since you seem so sure it was all down to his father...."

Win let his words drift off, and before he turned away, he saw the fear in her eyes, it was so strong he could almost smell it on her.

"Looks as though we need to start re-looking through the evidence with an eye on Mr. Peck being involved."

Win had addressed this to Brooks and Steph, who read his intentions perfectly and played along just as he'd hoped they would.

The two officers stood up and started gathering their belongings together, and Mrs. Peck unsuccessfully tried to hide her look of triumph at fooling them.

Once the officers were safely out of the house, she collapsed into one of the chairs and closed her eyes.

She'd pushed all thoughts of that night out of her head, but now the box she'd locked them in was open.

Getting out her phone she pressed her son's contact

"Terry, we need to talk. I think the police might be coming to see you, and I need to bring you up to date."

He was silent but she could hear him breathing into his end of the phone.

"I know you're still there Terry. Don't panic, I've got it all in hand, we just need to make sure we're singing from the same song sheet. I've never let you down, have I?"

Steph smiled, the other two had noisily slammed the front door closed while she'd hung around outside the kitchen door listening for Mrs. Peck's call.

It stood to reason that the first person she'd phone would be Terry, and they wanted to know what she'd say to him.

Creeping quietly down the hall she silently let herself out of the house.

The other two were leaning against the car waiting for her, at their questioning looks she nodded.

"Just as we thought, straight on the phone to Terry. She's planning to meet up with him later and update him, might be an idea for us to get there first?"

Win nodded, "Nice work Steph. Let's get straight over there and see what we can glean from Peck junior."

Chapter 19

Terry hung up the phone on his mother and kicked the leg of the table in frustration.

That's all he needed, the police asking questions.

He pulled on his shoes and stuck his keys in his pocket, better get straight over to his mum's and find out what she'd told them.

"Are you going out?"

Rachel's voice made him jump; he was so engrossed in his thoughts he'd forgotten she was home.

"What does it look like? I've put on my shoes and picked up my keys, so obviously I'm going out."

She gave him a hurt look, the one that irritated the shit out of him.

You'd think she'd have worked out by now that he had zero interest in how she felt, he thought.

Swallowing his annoyance, it wouldn't do to get her offside at the moment, he faked a contrite tone.

"Sorry love, I'm just all over the place. Yes, I'm going to see mum, check on how she is."

It seemed to have worked, but then she started looking for her own shoes

"I'll come with you. I can do a bit of cleaning or something for your mum. Help her out."

Terry could've cursed out loud, why the fuck didn't she get the hint?

"You know how mum gets with you, probably best I go on my own."

The hurt look was back at his reminder of how his mum felt about her.

He tried not to grin, his mum was always spiteful to his wife, no one was good enough for her boy, and Terry couldn't help but enjoy how she treated Rachel.

His joy at outsmarting his wife was short-lived.

He'd just picked up his wallet when the doorbell sounded, Rachel, glad of an escape from her snappy husband, rushed to answer it.

When the familiar voice of Win Phelps reached his ears, followed by the other two officers, he knew he wasn't going to get to his mum's before speaking to them.

Damn his stupid mother for not telling him everything over the phone so he was prepared, and while he was at it, damn his stupid wife for holding him up.

If she hadn't gone on and on at him earlier, he'd have been out of the house when the police got here.

The kitchen felt crowded with the five of them in it.

Without waiting to be invited, Win, Brooks, and Steph had taken up three of the seats around the table.

Terry had reluctantly taken the fourth, and Rachel was hovering around the doorway.

"I'll make everyone a drink, shall I?'

His wife was already making her way towards the kettle, but before Terry could put her off Win loudly took her up on her kind offer.

Thrown off-kilter and not in control as he usually was, Terry was silently fuming, but he was careful not to let that leak into his face or tone.

"What can I do for you all today? I was just off out to visit my mother, so I hope it won't take long. As you can imagine she's devastated at the loss of my father."

"I'm sure you both are," Win threw in.

Terry shot him a quick glance, but his face didn't give anything away.

Brooks now took over and Terry switched his attention to him.

"We've just come from your mother's actually; she seemed as good as expected under the circumstances so I'm sure she'll be fine while you give us a few minutes of your time."

Terry's blood was boiling with rage, but the only outward sign of his ill temper was the slight tremble to his hand as he picked up the mug of coffee his wife had just handed him.

Brooks continued as though he hadn't noticed.

"We found something very odd written on the mirror in the bathroom when we attended your dad's death. "You will all pay." Any idea what that might have meant?"

Terry knew he hadn't entirely hidden the shock he'd felt, but he decided it was probably the right reaction anyway.

"Seems a strange suicide note for him to leave?"

He put a question in his own voice, but he had a sinking feeling he knew exactly what the words referred to.

This time it was Steph that answered him, he was aware that they were dividing the questions up to try and throw him off but was determined to keep his cool.

"We don't think it was a suicide note, Terry. Do you think your dad might have been involved in anything that would've led to him or someone else writing that note on the mirror?"

Terry wanted time to think this through, he also needed to try and read their faces but if he did, they'd be even more suspicious.

He decided to play dumb, the important thing was to get them out of the house so he could find out what his mum had said earlier.

"No idea officers."

There was a heavy silence following his words, the three visitors seemed content to sip coffee and wait him out and Terry was equally as determined not to give them anything else.

It was broken by the ting of an email arriving on someone's phone, Brooks glanced down and then opened it.

He gave a smile when he saw the contents.

"Have a look at this for me please."

Without explaining further, he handed his phone to Terry who took it and scrutinised the image.

It was a blow-up of Willow Gardener, her small hand encased in Frank's, and his face in profile showed his mouth slightly open as though he was speaking to her.

In the far corner, almost out of shot, were the tips of a pair of trainers, non-descript trainers, the type everyone had in the 90s, but these had something different about them. Terry internally winced as he recognised the stupid bottle tops that he used to tie onto his laces to make him stand out.

Keeping his face and tone neutral he handed the phone back.

"Looks as though you finally have a breakthrough in the case officers. It's a shame Frank's dead."

Brooks didn't react to his bluntness.

"Someone told us that you used to decorate your trainers like that."

His thick finger tapped the pair of trainers as he spoke, Terry shrugged.

"A lot of us did. It was a bit of a thing. Could be anyone's feet in the corner of that photo, why would you think it was me?"

Win stepped in

"We heard that you, Frank, and George were inseparable, where one was you all were. Stands to reason that it's more likely to be your feet, doesn't it?"

"Not necessarily. Maybe it was George? We all got split up at one point that night, maybe George found Frank with Willow but for some reason never said anything when you questioned him."

"It's all very strange Mr. Peck. Of course, neither George nor Frank is able to answer any questions now. Did you ever suspect they had anything to do with Willow's disappearance?"

"If I'd have thought that I'd have told you at the time."

Terry's tone was sharp with anger and Win hid a grin at hitting his mark.

"Maybe your dad was involved too? That would explain the message on his mirror."

Steph had picked it up again now and Terry swiveled his head in her direction, she almost recoiled at the flash of disgust in his eyes.

He was clearly a man who didn't like to be questioned by a woman, she thought with interest.

"Did my mother say that?"

Win wasn't going to give him the satisfaction of an answer and ignored it by asking another question of his own.

"I wonder if you three did see Willow that night. Did you see her after she went missing Mr. Peck?"

Terry glared at him.

"If you've got an accusation to make just spit it out. Arrest me, charge me, or fuck off out of my house."

His angry outburst made his wife jump, and Win recognised the response of someone who was afraid of their partner.

He noted it to himself, potentially he could come back and talk to her when she was alone, maybe she'd be more likely to spill the beans on anything she knew.

Terry got to his feet, he'd locked his anger into a box and his voice was back to a calm and reasonable tone.

"If that's all I'm off to my mother's. I'd appreciate it if you left now."

The officers all stood, they didn't have enough to do anything, but his reactions had given them all something to think about.

"Give her our regards Mr. Peck. We'll probably be back with more questions."

They followed him to the door, and Terry waited until he'd made sure they were in their car and pulling away before getting in his own vehicle.

Win could see him in the rearview mirror, standing by the driver's door, staring at the back of their car, his face a mask of rage.

Chapter 20

Despite his temptation to get to his mother's as soon as he could, Terry resisted the urge to put his foot down. The last thing he needed right now was to be pulled over for speeding.

Who was it that was hounding them like this?

The only living people that knew were him and his mother now unless one of the others had told someone.

As that thought took hold, his heart sunk into his shoes, what if there was someone out there that knew everything?

The traffic lights ahead changed to red, and Terry dipped his clutch to drop gears ready to make a stop.

It all started smoothly enough, but when he went to press the brake, it wouldn't move.

It felt as though something was underneath it, causing resistance, and stopping it from working. It was spongy under his foot; he rammed his foot down harder but it didn't move an inch.

By this time, he was almost at the red light, and traffic was streaming across the road he was heading for.

As Terry grew closer and more desperate to stop his car, he started slamming his foot onto the brake over and over.

It was at this point he heard a childish giggle, and then a voice as light as the breeze.

"You will all pay."

Terry looked from side to side desperately, there was no way he could pull off the road and avoid shooting out onto the busy main road. He tried to twist the steering wheel, but that wouldn't move either.

Another giggle as something pressed down on the accelerator pushing his car to its full speed, and as he shot out of the turning straight into the oncoming traffic, he ducked his head into his hands.

He was briefly aware of the sound of his seatbelt being unclicked and the release of its pressure across his chest before the first vehicle hit him.

They hadn't reached Mrs. Peck when the police radio sprung to life.

An urgent voice was requesting all available units attend a serious road traffic incident.

"Witnesses are reporting the driver of a silver BMW is seriously injured, paramedics are in attendance."

Win tapped Steph on the shoulder.

"It might be a coincidence, but Terry drives a silver BMW and that's the route he'd take to his mother's"

Brooks cursed, "Shit."

Spinning the car around they headed back to the scene of the accident.

Everything was at a standstill when they arrived, cars, lorries, and buses were all stopped haphazardly across the road, and some of the occupants had got out and were walking around nosing at what was going on.

Unable to get by the pile-up, Brooks pulled over and they walked the few feet over to the cordon.

Flashing his badge at the uniform he got them all through and they headed to the center of the accident.

Fresh tire tracks crisscrossed the tarmac where the drivers had applied their brakes to try and avoid hitting another vehicle. A woman was sobbing somewhere among the wreckage and Win could hear a child screaming.

It was chaos.

Smoke and steam billowed from crumpled bonnets, and shattered glass littered the road.

The walking wounded were sat with paramedics and the more urgent cases were being wheeled into the back of ambulances.

Right in the middle of it all was a scrunched-up BMW.

The passenger's side was completely caved in, and the rear of the driver's side had taken a hard hit too.

The fire service was preparing the jaws of life and a paramedic had pushed themselves through the driver's side window to give emergency first aid to the patient.

Despite the swelling and damage to the driver's face Win immediately recognised him as Terry.

It looked as though the airbag had opened and caught him full in the face and chest.

A paramedic beckoned them to one side to give them an update.

"Witnesses are saying he just shot out in front of oncoming traffic after jumping the red light. From his injuries and what we've seen inside the car he wasn't wearing his seatbelt so even though the airbag deployed as it should he was flung into it with the force of the impact. We've only managed to do an initial examination of him through the window, we'll get a better look once the lid's off the car and we can get him out. We can see there's a lot of significant damage to his face, I'd guess fractures to his cheekbones, lacerations from the broken glass, and burns from hitting the airbag. He's in and out of consciousness and complaining of chest pain so possibly broken ribs too."

"Has he said anything about why he jumped the light straight into the traffic like that?"

The young woman shook her head

"He just keeps saying he couldn't stop. Maybe the car malfunctioned?"

Win was fairly sure that wasn't going to be the case but nodded anyway.

The paramedic lowered her voice, even though Terry was too far away to hear.

"Maybe it was a suicide attempt? From what we've heard from witnesses there was no attempt to brake."

The three of them thought that was unlikely, psychopaths like Terry were too narcissistic to even contemplate it, but again they kept it to themselves.

Brooks waited until the paramedic had trotted back off into the chaos before speaking.

"I think we should break the bad news to his mother."

Win nodded his agreement, but before they left, he walked over to the car's passenger side.

He lit himself a cigarette and toked on it while he checked out the car.

The glass had completely shattered out of the frame and he had a clear view of Terry.

He had to angle his body, so he didn't lean on any of the lethal-looking shards of metal while he peered through the window.

His neck was encased in a white brace, and his face was almost the same colour apart from a grey tinge.

Blood poured from gaping wounds across his face, but it was as Win's eyes moved higher that he realised the full extent of the damage that had been done.

A large shard of glass poked out from Terry's eye, blood had pooled around it and ran down his ruined face like red tears.

Turning away he nodded to the other two.

"Let's go."

Mrs. Peck looked down her long nose at them when she opened the front door.

Giving a deep sigh as though their very presence made her feel put upon, she waved them in.

"My son is on his way over; in fact, he should've been here by now. Is this going to take long?"

They waited until they were back in her kitchen before Brooks delivered the news, the colour drained out of her face and she collapsed heavily onto the spare chair, muttering over, and over.

"My boy, my beautiful boy."

Win got her a glass of water, placing it on the coaster in front of her he watched as she lifted it with a trembling hand.

The glass clattered against her teeth as she drank it back in large, thirsty gulps.

When it was empty, she tried to place it back on the coaster, but her hand was so shaky the glass caught the edge and tumbled to the hard-tiled floor.

It shattered into a hundred pieces, shards of glass skittering across the ground, but Mrs. Peck just stared blindly at it.

Win got up and fetched her dustpan and broom from the utility room, as he swept, she watched him warily.

Dumping the glass into the bin under the sink he put the implements back where he found them, and then leaned over her.

"It's time to talk Mrs. Peck. Terry's in a serious condition but it's likely he'll live this time; do you think he'll be as lucky next time?"

Her eyes darted wildly from side to side between the faces in front of her, and Brooks sighed.

"It's all over Mrs Peck. Whatever secret you've been hiding all these years, it's time for it to come out."

Her face collapsed, her usual haughty expression was replaced by one of vulnerability and fear, she nodded her agreement and taking a deep breath to steady her voice, she began.

Chapter 21

Her marriage had changed when Terry was born.

While she was expecting, her Arthur had been devoted to her, placing his large hand over her swelling stomach he'd enjoyed the feel of his child moving, and kicking inside his wife's belly.

They'd curled up on the sofa together, thinking of names and wondering if they'd have a girl or a boy.

Arthur had decorated the spare room so it became a nursery, and Elizabeth had spent hours finding all the things their new child would need.

She'd never forget how she felt when she saw him for the first time.

Bright red face scrunched up tight, and little fists balled in anger at being removed from his calm, quiet place in her womb, but to her, he was the most beautiful baby she'd ever seen.

She'd doted on him, responding to his every cry and mewl, never making her lovely boy wait for anything.

That's when she'd seen another side to Arthur and felt the jealousy he felt towards his own son.

It had started with small things, little digs and comments, and then outright complaints that she was still his wife.

"Let him cry, won't do the little snapper any harm and I need my tea."

At first, Elizabeth had tried to pacify him, making sure he had a hot meal ready when he came home and trying to ignore her son while she made banal conversation with the man she'd married.

Eventually, she couldn't do it anymore, Terry needed her more and he came first.

They'd argued about it, Arthur blustering and shouting her down, and one day he'd even raised his hand to her.

He hadn't hit her, he wasn't that sort of man, but the thought was there.

From that moment it all changed, for her, he wasn't who she'd thought he was, and for him, he felt as though he no longer had a role in his own home.

As Terry got older and started to speak, he commanded more and more of her time and attention.

He was liable to huge tantrums when he didn't get his way, screaming fits that went on so long he'd turn blue and leave Elizabeth afraid that he couldn't breathe.

Wiping away the tears with a soft hanky and murmuring soft platitudes until he calmed down, she'd be even more determined not to cause him any more distress.

The tantrums had stopped when he'd started school.

Instead, he'd show his disapproval with a cold, unrelenting silence that would fill the house with misery.

No amount of pleading and cajoling would bring him around until he was good and ready to forgive her.

He'd found it hard to make friends, too advanced for the other children, she'd decided as she stood alone outside the school gates waiting for him.

She'd heard the other parents complaining about him, jealousy was rampant, and they called him a bully just because he could hold his own in a fight.

She'd been pleased when he'd made friends with George and Frank, it showed how sensitive her Terry was, choosing friends who had problems like that.

George had a bully for a father and Frank was a tub of lard who was often mocked by the other children, but soon the three of them seemed thick as thieves.

Elizabeth ignored the teachers who tried to point out that Terry had "issues with social skills" especially that fawning, young woman who'd caused Arthur to give their son the belt. She'd never seen him so angry, and she'd been unable to stop him.

From then on it was as though it was just her and Terry in the house, she made sure that Arthur felt excluded and was pleased when he settled into his own routine of fishing and doing his own thing.

Everything rolled along just fine, right up until that night at the fair.

Some of what Elizabeth knew had come from Terry, some from after accounts of others, but at the time all she knew was that her son was in trouble and needed her.

Terry, George, and Frank had spotted Andy and his little sister as they headed toward the ghost train.

The little girl had been clutching an ugly, misshapen rabbit that looked as though it came from one of the stalls.

Terry had told her that Andy had been mean to Frank about how fat he was, and Terry was looking to even the score.

He'd pushed the smaller boy to the floor but instead of him fighting fair his friends had run over.

That rough boy from the council estate had threatened her Terry and he'd decided to back off rather than cause more problems.

That was her Terry, a boy who always tried to make the right choices.

It wasn't until a few minutes later that they spotted the little girl, Willow, heading off on her own in the direction of the toilet block.

Frank and George had suggested they have some fun, take her off for a while and frighten Andy.

Of course, those two had tried to suggest it was all Terry's idea later, but Elizabeth knew better.

When Terry had called his parents from the phone box, he'd sounded so calm, shock, she'd thought.

"There's been an accident and I think she's dead, mum."

She hadn't even asked who, Elizabeth had immediately sent his father, a mistake in hindsight, but she'd assumed he'd just know what to do.

He'd called her as soon as he'd seen what happened, incoherent and babbling about dead children. She'd ended up going out herself to help, her husband was a sniveling, trembling wreck, unable to do anything.

They'd moved her body to the outskirts of the fair by now, so she'd been able to get to them without needing to use the main entrance that the police were monitoring.

Marching through the woods, her torch beam bouncing across the ground, and her only concern for her son.

The little girl was lying on a bed of leaves and twigs under a tree, her head twisted unnaturally to one side and her skin as white as the moon.

Her face looked almost unmarked apart from the large, egg-shaped bump on her forehead, a lop-sided-looking stuffed rabbit lay next to her.

It was almost as though she was asleep, however, the lack of breath making her chest rise and fall was the main giveaway that she was dead.

She was only wearing a rainbow T-shirt and a pair of white knickers with lace trim around the legs and waist.

Elizabeth felt a wave of nausea, surely one of Terry's friends hadn't touched her in that way.

They were only children, she reassured herself, of course, they didn't do anything like that.

"What happened?"

They all stared at her, Frank was crying, with big, ungainly sobs and snot dripping out of his nose until he wiped it away with his cuff.

George looked as though he'd been turned to stone, his eyes wide and his mouth hanging open.

Her husband was glaring at Terry in silence, but Terry was the only one who seemed unaffected by it all.

"It was an accident mum. We were just going to play a prank on her brother and his friends."

Elizabeth eyed the body coldly, and then sent her gaze across the others standing around her.

"Which one of you is responsible?"

Frank's chest hitched as he tried to stop crying long enough to answer her.

"Terry reckoned it would be a good way to pay Andy back, we were just going to let him panic for a bit. Then Terry said we should cut her hair off and give her a scare, so we took her to the bathrooms and Terry used his knife to do it. She was struggling and crying, and I said we should just let her go."

Frank turned an accusing look at Terry.

"He didn't want to, he said she'd tell, and we'd all be in trouble. Terry told me to look away while he sorted it, I heard a thump and when I turned around, she was like that."

Elizabeth was one of the few people who could read Terry's micro-expressions, she knew immediately that Frank had told her the truth, but that was something she'd rather die than acknowledge.

It was the little smile that played on his lips, and the soft, dreamy look in his eyes as he remembered something he enjoyed.

Arthur was looking at his son in horror, as though Terry was a monster instead of his son.

This was going to be down to her, Elizabeth realised.

She was going to have to take charge, because if she didn't this could all land on Terry's head.

"We need to bury her. All of you have to help, and once it's done, we will never speak of it again is that clear?"

Using sticks and branches they made the grave as deep as they could, and then everyone stood back looking at it.

The hole was like a gash in the ground, dark with freshly turned soil. No one wanted to look at Willow, so again it fell to Elizabeth.

The child's eyes stared blankly at the canopy of branches above her, it was a beautiful night, the sky was like a sheet of black velvet spotted with twinkling stars.

The moon was full and bright, it lit the forest and turned Willow's skin to shimmering silver.

The child weighed little more than a pillow; Elizabeth lifted her carefully before laying her in the hole.

Now for the hardest part, covering the poor, dead child in dirt, burying her so that no one would ever find out what they'd done.

Terry was the first to move, he seemed to have no difficulty pushing the pile of soil back into the hole.

At first, Elizabeth watched, unable to tear her eyes away as black earth was scattered across Willow's face.

Her gaze met Arthur's, but the look of despair, and disgust on his face made her look away.

Then finally, it was over.

All that was left was the mound of soil covering her little body, they worked silently, smoothing out the ground and using moss and branches to hide the freshly dug grave.

The five of them all left together, creeping through the woods to the town beyond, but before they went their separate ways,

Elizabeth gave them a final word of warning.

"No one must tell, if you do, then we will all go to prison. This is our secret now, and we shall take it to our graves.

Win wasn't fooled by Elizabeth's red-rimmed eyes, or contrite tone, her cheeks were dry, and she hadn't shed a single tear.

Like mother, like son, he thought.

This was a woman who'd buried a small girl in the woods, who'd let her family rip themselves apart not knowing what had happened to her, all to protect her psychopath son.

In fact, the only reason she was talking now was because she hoped it would save him.

"Can you show us where she is?"

Brooks asked the question they all wanted the answer to, and Elizabeth nodded.

"I'll never forget, so yes, I can show you where she is."

They'd headed straight over, no more time to waste, thought Win, he would finally be able to give Willow's family closure.

As soon as she'd pointed to the spot, Steph had clapped on the cuffs, read her rights, and bundled her off to a nearby police car to be taken to the station.

The forensic team was there quickly and Win contacted Andy to let him know before it became a headline on the news.

He must have got in touch with his mother as the both of them stood together, sharing a large brolly against the rain that had started beating down almost as soon as they'd got to the woods.

Forensics had put up one of those white evidence tents so they could work in the dry and away from prying eyes.

They were slow and meticulous, and it was over an hour before they got to her.

The small skeleton was still wearing the remains of her bright, rainbow T-shirt, and a dirty, ragged stuffed rabbit was buried next to her.

Win stood with the Gardners, as the small black body bag was bought out.

By now Andy's father had also arrived and for the first time in a long time, they stood as a small family unit watching as the youngest member was finally returned to them.

Chapter 22

Terry was aware that he'd been charged with murder, and the knowledge of that fact also came with the awareness of why.

His mother.

Apparently, the stalwart of the family, the only person he thought he could trust had told the police the whole sordid tale after his "accident."

When he'd first awoken from the induced coma, they'd given him no more than a couple of hours to come round before showing up to read him his rights.

DCI Brooks and his sidekick, DS Wright, could barely hide their distaste for him, alongside their self-righteous enjoyment.

The nurses were no less professional, but he could sense their discomfort at being in his room, they touched him only when treatment necessitated, and even then, it was done as quickly as possible.

It had taken another week before his wife had come by, seven days of no visitors, while he could hear the other patients receiving theirs.

He was in a room of his own, not because he was held in special regard, but because no one wanted to share a room with a child killer.

Rachel had slipped into his room quietly; she hadn't even pushed the door fully open before easing herself through.

A quick look over her shoulder suggested she was checking that no one had seen her come in, her shame at visiting him so obvious even he could read it.

Her brown hair was scraped back in a messy bun, and the dark rings under her puffy eyes suggested it had been a while since she last slept a full night.

Hovering around next to his bed, her face drawn and serious, she announced the real reason for being there. No "how are you?" or "Do you need anything?"

No flowers, cards, or baskets of fruit, just the bald, blunt statement that she was starting the process for divorce.

Incapacitated, and trapped in his hospital bed he'd silently fumed whilst keeping his blank mask securely on his face.

A face that no longer looked like his own.

The staff wouldn't give him a mirror, they'd removed the one from the adjoining bathroom and discouraged him from looking at himself.

"Wait until you've healed a little more Mr. Peck. It'll look worse than it is right now."

Terry wasn't one to take advice, and it hadn't been difficult to swipe the small compact with mirror out of a nurse's pocket when she was leaning over to change his drip.

Flicking it open he bought the small mirror as close as he could, it wasn't big enough to show him his whole face at once, so he checked each part bit by ugly bit.

At first, it hadn't seemed so bad, his chin and lower face looked relatively unscathed, some grazes and nicks but nothing that wouldn't heal eventually.

It was as he moved up that he realised how bad it was, a long wending scar traveled along his right cheek, angry red and thick as a garden worm.

Worse than that, however, was the furrow that spread across his left cheek and onto his nose, a deep gouge out of his flesh that left that side of his face hollow like a man missing his teeth.

The most horrific injury was yet to come though, moving the mirror up, his left eye was covered by a gauze square fixed in place by clear tape.

Picking back the edges of the tape he gingerly pulled it back so he could see underneath it.

Puckered skin sunk his eye socket back into his skull, his eye was gone and in its place was a raw, empty cavity.

Rachel flinched when he turned towards her, he'd initially given her his less ruined right side and the shock of seeing the full glory of his new face had drained what colour she had left.

He forced himself to shrug, he wanted to smash his fist into her face but as that wasn't possible, he'd rather she think he couldn't care a less.

"I'm guessing you don't want a monster for a husband?"

He was referring to his injuries, but when she replied it was clear that she was distancing herself from the recent revelations.

"It's not what you look like Terry, I want to make that clear. It's what you did and who you are."

Reaching into her large shoulder bag she dumped the local paper on his bed, announced he'd be hearing from her lawyer, and left the room as silently as she'd entered it.

The headline shouted at him from its place on his legs, alongside it was a photo of him pre-accident.

"LOCAL HEADMASTER CHARGED WITH MURDER OF MISSING WILLOW GARDNER"

He was sure if he could be bothered to read it, he'd find photos of the crime scene and anonymous quotes from staff and pupils claiming they'd always thought there was something about him.

Everyone wanted their five minutes of fame, and this was a big deal in a small town where nothing usually happened.

Flopping back against his pillows he stared at the ceiling, the nurse had promised him a book to read but hadn't bothered coming back with one.

It had happened in increments that night, one choice leading to another, and ending in only one option.

When he'd spotted Willow, the thought had popped into his head as though it had been waiting for an opportunity.

He'd turned to Frank and George, nudging them and then pointing at her.

She'd been skipping, he remembered that her mouth had been moving as she sang to herself, swinging that ugly rabbit in her hand, lost in her own world.

Frank had approached her first, the photo had captured the moment he'd taken her small hand and whispered reassurances that he'd help her find her toilets.

The trusting little kid had happily grasped the older boy's hand, babbling about her brother as they headed towards the collection of portaloos.

She hadn't looked afraid until Terry and George had appeared, even then she'd seemed more confused than anything else.

No one had argued with his idea to cut off those stupid bouncing, blonde curls, although he'd seen George pale as he'd pulled out his penknife.

She'd cried, screamed, and fought him as hard as she could, he'd almost admired her guts.

When he'd told Frank he was worried that she'd tell, to turn around while he sorted it, he'd made out it was just the way it had turned out.

Truth was, Terry had planned this all along, from the moment he'd seen her holding her brother's hand and looking at him with admiring eyes.

He didn't know why but he felt the need to destroy what others loved and seeing the affection between them he'd known that if he had a chance, he'd snuff it out.

He'd broken her neck.

Being so little it hadn't been much more of a challenge than the neighbourhood cats he'd killed.

She'd banged her stupid head on the sink though, blood smearing the white porcelain and running down her red shorts.

They'd dragged her out, ripping her shorts off and handing them to George to dispose of before carrying her into the woods out of sight.

Terry had planned to go back and clean up the bathroom but by the time he'd dumped her off with his friends, the police were already there.

Instead, he'd called his mother, and of course, she'd sorted it for him.

He'd had another moment of panic when he realised that George had just tossed the shorts to one side and that Andy's friend had found them, but then he reassured himself that it might be for the best.

They'd suggest that a pervert had got her, stripped her, and taken her away, maybe dressed her as a boy what with the hair in the sink.

For thirty years he'd put it all away in a locked box in his head, no one seemed to think about her anymore, the police had iced the case and Terry was scot-free.

A cold draught tickled his ear, it was as gentle as a breath.

Terry moved his head and noticed that the machines that monitored his vitals had all shut down, where there'd been glowing green digits and persistent beeps there was now nothing.

He reached for the call button to alert the staff, but no amount of pushing seemed to work.

Giving a huff of irritation he tossed it down on the covers, as soon as he heard someone walk by outside, he'd have to call out for them.

Terry flinched as the cold draught blew past his ear again, but this time it carried whispered words from a small childlike voice.

"You will all pay."

It was suddenly difficult to catch his breath, his heart pounded, and the blood rushed in his ears.

He felt a stabbing pain in his chest, so sharp it was as though a knife had been pushed through his ribs.

Terry could hear the stale air rattling in his lungs, he couldn't push it out and he couldn't drag in the fresh oxygen he needed.

With the machines not functioning no alert was being sent to the nurse's station.

The vision in his one good eye was clouding over, like a mist on an early morning in summer, and then he heard a faint, delighted giggle.

At the nurse's station, Brenda tried to take the weight off her aching feet by leaning on the desk and lifting them one at a time.

It didn't help much, she was in need of a long soak in the bath with a book, and maybe a glass of cold white wine.

"Bren, can you pop your head around Mr. Peck's room, please? Sorry to ask, but I've got a giant-sized list of obs to do and he's due a check."

Brenda nodded and resisted the urge to sigh, they were all keeping it as professional as possible, but any time spent with the child killer chilled her blood.

To think he was just a kid himself when he did it, she mused.

Steeling herself to conceal the disgust under her work expression, she raised her hand and tapped lightly on the door.

When there was no reply, she was relieved, she could nip in and check on him without the need to have any conversation.

Pushing the door open she crept in, he looked asleep at first glance from the doorway with his hand flopped outside of the bars of his hospital bed.

It was only when she got closer, she noticed his one remaining eye was wide open and staring at her disconcertingly.

The eye was already starting to film over, and no breaths moved the sheet covering him.

Brenda noticed the machines were off, hence why no alert had come through to the nurse's station.

She checked his pulse, already sure there wouldn't be one, and not surprised when it confirmed what was already obvious.

She tried to find even a small kernel of sadness at his loss, but even in her caring nurse's heart, there was nothing.

Elizabeth Peck was as despised as her son.

The news of his death had been shared with cold dispassion by the prison governor who'd peered over her glasses at the prisoner in front of her.

"Can I attend the funeral?"

The governor, an austere woman in her late fifties had flicked her a disapproving glance.

"Can I attend the funeral Ma'am, is the correct way to address me. And no, the home office has already made it clear that you are not going to be able to attend due to security concerns. The number of death threats against you gives credible rise to a risk to your life."

Elizabeth had begged and pleaded but to no avail.

"I don't care, my life isn't worth living without him, I just want to say goodbye to my son."

The governor sighed deeply and shook her head.

"We'd be in the firing line if anything happened to you so it's not a choice you get to make."

Clearly finished with the conversation she motioned to the burly female guard waiting next to her.

Travis had a face like a bulldog licking piss off a thistle, her mouth was a stern, unrelenting line under the puffy pouches of her flabby face.

She'd grasped Elizabeth's arm and propelled her out of the office on wobbling legs, she wasn't able to offer any resistance, it was as though all her strength had seeped out of her when she'd heard the news.

They'd put her on suicide watch, which seemed to involve a guard regularly staring at her through the open shutter on her cell door.

No one asked how she was, it was just their job to make sure she didn't top herself on their watch.

Mealtimes were the worst, the guards escorted her to the dining room, stood over her while she got her food, and then took her back to eat it alone in her single cell.

They didn't intervene when other prisoners jostled her, poked her, and called her a murdering bitch.

"My kiddie's only five too you murdering piece of shit. I'm going to shank you bitch, slice your ugly face."

The angry woman leered her face as close to Elizabeth's as she could without actually touching her.

From behind someone drove a hand into the middle of her back shoving her forward and almost knocking her off her feet.

The angry shouting woman jumped back as though touching Elizabeth would make her sick.

A laugh from one side suggested that the women were enjoying the sport, Elizabeth kept her face guarded and didn't show her fear.

Inside her stomach churned and fear fluttered like butterflies, if these women ever got their hands on her she wouldn't bet on her survival.

So long as no one got overtly physical the guards seemed content to let her get her share of the bile and hatred that spewed her way.

The death threats from outside the prison were picked up before they even reached her, but the guards ensured she knew the contents anyway.

Travis took a special delight in giving her chapter and verse when she was on duty.

Letting herself into the single cell she'd prop her stubby body against the doorframe and pull the letters out of her pocket. Making a show of reading through them to herself before quoting them out loud to her captive audience.

"You got a humdinger yesterday, Peck. Nice and short and to the point it was, this one wants five minutes alone with you to make sure you get what's coming to you. Mention of a knife and a baseball bat. Not as vivid as the one that offered to carve you into small pieces and flush the remains down the loo though. What's it like to be one of the most hated women in the country?"

Elizabeth had ignored her, what was the point in responding? It was a stupid question anyway.

"Not feeling very chatty today, Peck?"

Travis shrugged, "I'm off to my chair outside where I get to spend a few hours staring at your door and hoping you don't off yourself while I'm there."

The grief at the loss of her son had been overwhelming, and if she could've found a way to end it all she would've.

All she had left was years, and years locked away in this prison or another just like it, hated by all and isolated by their disgust.

A dull thud from outside in the hall made her jump, the prison was full of noises, screams, shouts, crying, and crashing, but this was right outside her cell.

She heard the jangle of keys that preceded a guard letting themselves in and she prepared herself for another round of "guess who wants to kill you" with a gloating Travis.

However, it wasn't Travis she saw when the door eased open, it was the woman from the canteen. The shouty, angry one who wanted to cut her face to ribbons.

Behind her were another two women, she recognised the tall, gangly one known as Frannie and the small, stout one with the shaved head who went by the name "Lady." All of them held something in their hands, Lady had her trademark sock filled with a heavy snooker ball nicked from the rec room, and Frannie had a toothbrush shaved into a sharp point.

The first woman in, Elizabeth was sure she'd heard someone call her Yvonne, looked empty-handed at first.

It wasn't until she was right inside the cell that she produced a mug from behind her back.

All three stared at her silently for a moment, Elizabeth, frozen to the spot, shuddered when she felt a wisp of cold air pass by her right ear. It felt like someone was whispering to her but she couldn't make out the words.

"Well, well, baby killer. Guess what I've got here?"

"I'm starting to doubt it's a nice cup of earl grey."

At her sarcastic retort the three women moved a step closer, steam was rising from the cup in Yvonne's hand.

"I'm not sure there's anything nice about it bitch, not unless you're keen on boiling water laced with as much sugar as we could get our hands on."

Boiling sugar, the punishment traditionally handed out in women's prisons to those accused of hurting or killing children.

Elizabeth took another step back, but this time she felt the wall behind her, there was no further to go, and the three women were blocking the only exit.

No sign of Travis either, which meant that she was either in on it or incapacitated.

Yvonne went first, as the one who'd initiated the plan, she got first dibs.

The boiling sugar clung to Elizabeth's face as it scalded through the layers of skin and flesh right through to the bone. At first, the pain had been excruciating, but as the nerves died so did the worst of the pain.

There was no such luxury when the other two joined in though, she felt every slice as Frannie carved patterns in her flesh, and it was almost welcome when Lady used the sock.

DCI Brooks leaned back in his chair; he spun in a slow circle as he thought about what he'd just read. The email had been factual, cold, and bland, but ultimately it would appear that the Pecks had been wiped off the face of the planet.

Steph didn't have to wait long for his comment, he smiled at her as he shrugged.

"Looks like it's all over Wright. Terry had an aneurism, air in his drip or something, and then his mum got done over in prison last night. Three prisoners managed to take out the guard, steal her keys, and access Mrs. Peck's cell. They made a right mess of her, the boiling sugar trick, then another one sliced her up, and a snooker ball in a sock to batter her with."

He gave a sly smile.

"I've got a mate who works there, he reckons she was unrecognisable when they finally got to her. They'd caved her whole head in, and that's without the damage to her face from the boiling sugar and the shank. The three women just sat calmly outside the cell waiting for the guards, they didn't care about being hauled up for it either. One of them said that they'd be heroes anyway. Never underestimate how much female prisoners hate a child killer I guess."

Steph couldn't seem to find a feeling beyond relief, she wanted to feel more, the woman must have suffered terribly before she died, but all she could see was the small skeleton of a little girl in a rainbow T-shirt clutching the lopsided rabbit her big brother had won her at the hoopla.

"So, do you think that's it?"

Oliver nodded, "Frank, George, and the Peck family were all involved in her abduction, killing, and burial and they're all gone. That Gardner woman, all I can think is that maybe it was to stop her going back to the papers about Andy's visit. We can't credit Cleo and Willow herself for this solve but those of us in the know are aware of why we finally got to the truth."

Steph sighed, "Hopefully, the poor little mite is at peace now, and giving her family closure might help them get their lives back."

Brooks hoped so, but with the loss of a child, could there ever be peace of mind again?

Chapter 23

It was fitting that the sky was overcast and grey, thought Andy, and so it should be on the day we finally lay my little sister to rest.

The church had been packed, everyone in town had shown up to pay their respects and he'd shaken so many hands he'd lost count.

The front pew was for the small family of three that Willow had once belonged to and behind him the outsiders with honorary member Cleo.

Andy sat between his parents, Mark on his left, his face haggard and drawn, looking as though he'd aged twenty years in the last week since Willow was found.

His mother on his right, although careworn, she looked lighter, as though the closure had given her inner peace.

After the service, he'd shaken more hands and thanked people he barely remembered for coming.

There'd be no wake, no dried-up sandwiches and cold sausage rolls handed out to the guests, this was the only part of it they planned to share.

Her burial would be for family and close friends only, and the remembrance of her life would also be restricted to the small inner circle that had known and loved her.

It started to rain as they stood around the hole in the ground in the churchyard, it was a small grave for a little girl who was taken too soon.

It was still summer, and the rain was a light, warm sprinkle rather than a cold deluge.

His parents stood together, his father's new family and his own wife and daughter huddled together away from them. His stepmother was a kind, generous woman who'd graciously given Mark and Jilly the space to grieve their child together. Not only that, but she was supporting his wife and daughter too.

His friends, Derek, Steve, and Evan stood with Win, Brook, and Steph in a semi-circle.

Cleo was the closest one to him, but Andy had left a gap between him and everyone else. He'd noticed her reaching out and brushing Evan's hand every now and again. Although he was pleased for his friends, he didn't have it in him to wish them well.

He didn't want any contact with anyone, his stomach churned and twisted like a washing machine.

The guilt was stronger now than it had ever been, she'd be alive today if it wasn't for him letting go of her hand.

Mucking about with his friends, fighting with those stupid kids, he'd let her down.

Win had gently told him the whole story; he felt the bile rise as he imagined her fear that night.

A boy her brother's age had sliced off her beautiful curls with a knife before snapping her neck and tossing her away as though she was nothing.

He hated himself for it, but he was glad Terry and his bitch mother were dead, he hoped they were in hell.

The anger he felt was so unlike him it still shocked him with its intensity. He was turning into his mother, he thought, bitter, angry, and hateful.

It looked as though it was brightening up, he thought sourly as a sharp ray of light made him shade his eyes.

He shook his head to clear the fog that he felt seeping in, it was as though his ears had popped, and everything sounded distant and blurred.

A tap on his shoulder made him look over to his right, Cleo was smiling at him, her face was as clear as her words, but when she spoke it wasn't her voice he heard.

"Andy. Please don't be sad anymore. It wasn't your fault."

No matter that it had been over thirty years since he heard it, he'd know Willow's voice anywhere.

The light touch on his cheek bought tears to his eyes, it felt as though a small fingertip was tracing his face.

"I love you, Andy."

The voice was no more than a whisper and the brush of cold lips was just the merest sensation.

A warm feeling of peace flooded him, he felt the darkness of guilt, self-loathing and grief lift like a heavy blanket thrown off on a hot night.

He slowly became aware that the light was gone, the day was still grey and overcast, but across the horizon, he could see the start of a blue sky.

His mum tucked her arm around his left side and squeezed, her eyes were clear and shone with love.

"Let's get back to Derek's, shall we? It was so kind of him to offer to lay everything on for us at his house. I'm looking forward to getting to know my beautiful granddaughter."

Her voice softened, and she leaned into his ear so no one else could hear.

"I'm sorry Andy. It was as though I was lost in the dark and I couldn't see you anymore. She spoke to me too you know; she told me it wasn't your fault, and I didn't realise until then that I'd been blaming you as much as myself. I was just so filled with anger and bitterness; I know I've missed so much...."

She broke off as her voice cracked

Andy cupped his mum's face in his hand, and just before they were interrupted by the squeals of Lissie approaching, he could've sworn he felt a small cold hand over his.

Smiling to himself he took hold of his daughter's little hand, and the family headed out of the cemetery together.

Afterword

I'd like to thank you for reading "Willow Weeps."

As an Indie Author, every reader is much appreciated, but if I can ask one more favour of you, it would be to leave a review.

I also love to hear your suggestions and feedback personally, so please find my on social media as @MgarciaAuthor or contact me through my website.

If you would like updates on new releases and giveaways please consider following me or subscribing to my blog.

Books By This Author

Breach of Trust

When someone starts killing men on the sex offenders registers Adam & Sarah have their work cut out whittling down the suspect list. The problem is, no one suspect has the means, motive, and opportunity for all the murders. Can they get to the truth before more people die?

Bedding Down

The brutal assault and murder of a homeless man lead the team into the local community of rough sleepers. They'll have to dig deep into the past to find out what the link is, can they identify the killer before there's another murder? In a case that brings back difficult memories for one of the team, and we learn more about Carpy's friend Big Bill. Four men have been protecting a secret for the last ten years, but keeping it is going to cost them their lives.

Becoming Bill

Bill is a fictional character, but his experiences of homelessness and rough sleeping are a grim reality for many. I've worked in homelessness for many years and his story is a combination of the things I've heard. It's a story that may make you cry, but it's also full of hope and of lessons learned. Maybe this book will make you see the next rough sleeper you pass differently. Over 50% of all UK rough sleepers have a significant and enduring mental health diagnosis, and even worse over 85% will experience being assaulted or abused while on the streets. This is a book for readers who have an interest in social awareness as well as an enjoyable read. Will Bill have the courage to face his past and start again?

Tales of Darkness Drive

Part of the Twisted Tales Series of horror short story collections.

Deadly fog, and journeys to unexpected places. Darkness Drive is a place where the residents have a unique way of dealing with problem neighbours.

Comeuppance

Part of the Twisted Tales series of horror short story collections.

Travel to a world where karma rules and those who deserve it always get their comeuppance.

Don't miss out!

Visit the website below and you can sign up to receive emails whenever Molly Garcia publishes a new book. There's no charge and no obligation.

https://books2read.com/r/B-A-VETV-DKLHC

BOOKS 2 READ

Connecting independent readers to independent writers.